# The SEAL Next Door

## AN ALPHA SEALS NOVEL

Makenna Jameison

ISBN: 9781718027701

# Table of Contents

# Chapter 1

Matthew "Gator" Murphy breathed in the humid Florida air as he strode down the ramp of the C-17 military cargo plane, duffle bag gripped tightly in his right hand. His muscles flexed with the movement, and he ground his jaw as the bright sunlight blinded him.

He ran his hand through his dark, short cropped hair, instinctively realizing his helmet was missing. *Scratch that.* He sure the hell didn't need it here on U.S. soil.

Slipping on his aviators, he walked across the tarmac on Pensacola Naval Base like he owned the place. You'd been on one military base, you'd been on them all. And with his current frame of mind, he didn't give a damn what Commanders or Admirals were wandering around. He was in a mood to kick ass and take names.

The dampness in the air clung to his skin, making

him feel like he'd walked out of the climate-controlled interior of the plane and straight into a sauna. The gentle breeze blowing in from the Gulf did little to cool down the air temperature—or his current mood. A few palm trees swayed in the distance next to the administration building, but the rest of the place was standard military: miles of concrete, men and women in uniform, rows upon rows of planes.

He felt strange walking around in civilian gear, but for once, he wasn't hopping a ride on a transport to head overseas on an op. Most of his SEAL team buddies were back where he'd left them in Little Creek. His gear was stashed away at his apartment in Virginia.

Home sweet home was his final destination today.

"Sir," a junior officer said as he passed, saluting him.

Matthew saluted in return, a feeling of pride surging through him, temporarily replacing his anger. Even without his uniform on, he commanded attention. At 6'4" with the brawny build of a SEAL, he was used to the stares of civilians. But hell if it didn't feel good to have others in the military show him the respect he'd earned. The acknowledgement he deserved. At thirty, he'd devoted twelve years of his life to the U.S. Navy. And when a junior officer noticed his seniority, despite his lack of uniform, well didn't that feel fucking nice.

"Do you know where I can find Colton Ferguson?" Matthew asked the junior officer.

"Yes, sir. He's inside the admin building over there. Second office on the left."

"Thank you." Matthew nodded and continued on his way.

Any other time he might have welcomed the brief respite from his duties as a SEAL stationed in Little Creek, Virginia. Part of an elite six-member team that was frequently deployed on missions all over the globe, he worked hard and played harder. Drilled on the water, did daily PT with his men, trained even in his off hours, and chased after the pretty girls on the weekend. And hell. Who wouldn't enjoy a weekend back at home? A few days on the Gulf, down by the beach, far away from work?

Except the emergency leave granted so that he could attend his best friend's homecoming from Walter Reed Medical Center wasn't exactly part of the plan.

Not this weekend.

Not fucking ever.

Best friends since childhood, Beckett Miller had been like the brother he never had. With Beckett's younger sister Brianna trailing after them, the three of them had enjoyed childhood adventures traipsing around the marshland, taking their small boat out on the water, and sneaking off to the beach after dark. Beckett had enlisted in the Navy right out of high school just like Matthew.

Although Beckett was also a SEAL, he was based out of Coronado. An ambush late one night on a highway in the remote part of Afghanistan, serving his duty to Uncle Sam, had left his friend comatose for more than a month and missing one leg.

Hell. What was he supposed to say to Beckett's parents? To Beckett himself? To Beckett's sister? He hadn't even seen Brianna in years. Maybe they'd been inseparable in childhood, but today he wouldn't know the woman if she smacked right into him. Matthew had enlisted in the Navy at age eighteen. Between BUD/S out in Coronado, missions all over the world, and his current station near Virginia Beach, he had little time to spend at home. He couldn't even recall the exact date he'd last been back.

Four years his and Beckett's junior, Brianna had just been starting high school when he'd left. Then she'd gone off to college, started her own career, and the years had slipped away. He thought he remembered Beckett saying she was back in Florida, working on some type of marketing gig. Temporarily living with her parents again.

Damn.

Seeing Beckett's family would just bring up more memories of their childhood. Of a time when Beckett wasn't injured and the world was theirs to conquer and explore.

With the way Matthew's gut was currently churning, he didn't think he could deal with the onslaught of memories about the life that once was. Of the future his best friend now faced. No more active duty. No more life as a SEAL. Beckett could find a desk job, sure, but guys like them were meant to be in the thick of it. To jump out of airplanes, dive in the ocean, tote around weapons, battle foreign adversaries. To see action. To camp out in the desert and haul around eighty-pounds of gear on their backs.

But with one leg? Even though Beckett could lead a normal civilian life from here on out, life as he knew it with the SEALs was over.

Fucking hell.

Matthew needed to get through this weekend and move on. Get back to life in Little Creek and his men. His missions. Tuck the pain and grief of nearly losing his best friend so far away that it never saw the light of day again. Seeing Beckett was going to be gut-wrenching. Seeing Beckett's parents and sister would be worse. Matthew was a SEAL that had survived countless missions with barely a scrape. Who had convinced his best friend to enlist in the Navy right along beside him. How was he supposed to look them in the eye knowing he had what Beckett never would again? A long career in the military, all his limbs, a normal civilian life once he eventually retired.

The guilt was nearly eating him alive.

And seeing Brianna again after all these years?

Hell.

The little girl in pigtails he'd palled around with as a kid was long gone. She was barely a teenager when he'd enlisted in the Navy. And although he hadn't missed those puppy dog eyes she'd cast upon him every now and then as they'd grown older, he was a red-blooded American male, interested in the older college girls. The co-eds with womanly figures, plenty of tempting curves, and legs that went on for miles. Not some scrawny young girl who'd been almost like a sister to him. Who he'd never see as anything other than the girl next door.

What would it be like facing her now all these years later? He felt like he'd let her down as much as anyone—convincing her brother to join the Navy. Become a SEAL. Lose a leg and nearly die.

Sweat broke out across his brow as the guilt once again churned in his stomach.

"Yo, Gator, wait up!" Evan "Flip" Jenkins, one of the men on his SEAL team, called out from behind. "Gator" was the nickname Matthew had earned back in BUD/S since he was from Florida. It was kind of ironic now since he hardly ever set foot in the state, but the name had stuck throughout his years in the Navy.

He glanced back to see Evan jogging up behind him, his short blond hair reflecting the bright sunlight. Evan tucked his phone back into his cargo pants.

"Flip, what's up?" Matthew asked.

"What time's Beckett flying in from Walter Reed?"

"Sunday at three. Why? Is the CO already expecting us back?"

"Nah, nothing like that. Some of the other guys may come down for it."

Matthew paused. The men on his team were a close-knit group, more like blood brothers than comrades. They had each other's backs both on and off the battlefield and could practically move as one unit, training and fighting together. The only guy he'd ever been closer to was Beckett. And hell, he'd known him since they were kids. But to have his SEAL team fly down for the arrival of a wounded warrior? A fellow SEAL? That was unexpected. Not to mention damn welcome.

He'd seen more casualties in war than he ever cared to—injured soldiers, innocent civilians who'd been maimed, men killed in battle. But someone he'd known his entire life? Who he barely had a childhood memory without? That shit cut deep.

Matthew cleared his throat. "I'd really appreciate it. Beckett is like family to me. And he's a fellow SEAL."

"He's a good man," Evan agreed. "I wasn't stationed with him long, but hell, it's an honor to welcome home another SEAL. Not every man is lucky enough to come back from the warzone alive."

"Damm straight," Matthew agreed.

Evan himself had been critically injured on a mission several months ago. He'd done his time in Walter Reed and was lucky enough to be able to return to active duty. Beckett may never run ops again as a SEAL, but it was a miracle he had survived. Now if Matthew could just remember that every time he felt sorry for himself. For Beckett. For having to watch his friend go through that shit.

"Do the guys need us to make arrangements for a place for them to stay?" Matthew asked.

"Nah, they're on it. The CO can't let everyone come. Cobra's flying down tomorrow," he said, referring to Brent "Cobra" Rollins, another man on their SEAL team. "Maybe Ice," he added, referring to their team leader Patrick "Ice" Foster.

"It's good of you guys to come. Drinks are on me tomorrow night."

Evan chuffed out a laugh. "They damn well better be. Ali's giving me shit about leaving."

Matthew raised his eyebrows. The carefree nurse Evan had been dating and was now living with enjoyed laughing and joking with all the men on their SEAL team. She was always up for grabbing a beer and shooting the shit with the rest of them. Getting upset over Evan being gone didn't sound like her. Not when they deployed all the damn time anyway.

"Everything okay?" Matthew asked.

Evan cleared his throat. "Yeah, uh, we haven't really told anyone yet, but Ali's pregnant."

"Holy shit," Matthew said.

*Pregnant.*

*Holy hell.*

"Uh, congratulations?" Kids were the last thing on

Matthew's mind. Not to mention girlfriends, long-term relationships, and the idea of ever settling down with one woman for life. That worked for some dudes, but as for Matthew? He'd come to terms long ago with the fact that he was better off alone. Permanently.

Evan guffawed. "It was a surprise, but a good thing. A great thing," he added, and Matthew could hear the pride in his voice. "None of the other guys know yet," Evan continued, "so keep it on the down-low for now. I have to figure out how to break the news to them."

"Roger that," Matthew said with a grin. Hell. The other guys would likely give Evan plenty of grief. They ribbed each other like brothers, and with Evan being the youngest guy on the team, he often got the worst of it. But damn, if Evan and Ali were happy, then so was Matthew. For them at least. He wasn't gonna touch the idea of settling down with a woman or raising a family with a ten-foot pole.

"Next time you talk to Ali, give her my congratulations."

"Will do. She might kill me at the moment though with how sick she's been, but I'll tell you, that woman is over-the-moon happy."

Matthew laughed. "Hell, you and Ali will make great parents."

"I'm convinced it's a girl," Evan admitted. Matthew raised his eyebrows. "It's way too soon to tell," Evan quickly added, "but I've got a gut feeling. After all the hell I raised as a kid, I guess it serves me right. I'm going to have to worry about all the boys chasing after her when she's a teenager."

"Damn. That means I'm never, ever having a kid,"

Matthew muttered. "Karma's a bitch."

Evan's phone buzzed, and he held it up for Matthew to see, miming a slicing motion across his throat. Alison's name flashed across the screen.

"Let me talk to her," Matthew said. Evan answered and then passed him the phone.

"Congratulations, darlin'," Matthew drawled.

"I'm going to kill Evan for knocking me up!" Alison wailed. "I've been sick all day long. I know that's normal—I'm a nurse for God's sake. But do I really have to survive only on saltines and ginger ale for the next nine months?"

"Aw, hell, sweetheart. That boy is practically grinning from ear-to-ear right now at the idea of being a dad. Do you need me to rough him up a little or something? Maybe if I punch him in the gut he'll get sick, too. Would that make you feel better?"

Alison weakly laughed. "Don't you dare touch him, Matthew!"

Matthew smirked. "Wouldn't dream of it. Let me put boy wonder back on."

He handed the phone back to Evan, shaking his head, and began walking toward the administration building. Evan trailed behind him, finishing up his call. A year ago every man on the team had been single. Now, save for himself and Brent, the other four guys were all playing happily ever after with their girlfriends. Un-fucking-believable. His SEAL team leader Patrick and his girlfriend Rebecca each had kids from previous relationships, but the other guys were kid-free. Now Evan and Alison were adding a baby to the mix of their group of friends?

*Damn.*

Life was moving on at a wicked pace without him.

Before long the rest of those guys would probably be married and looking to find a less dangerous career. Not that he blamed them. Life as a SEAL made it tough to maintain any semblance of a relationship, which was part of the reason he was still single. But it worked for him. Suited him. And if he ever did happen to meet a woman he was willing to give it all up for? Well, he'd cross that bridge if and when he came to it. Which was likely not ever gonna happen.

Pushing open the heavy door to the admin building, a blast of AC rushed over his heated skin. It felt pretty damn amazing. Pushing his aviators atop his head, he strode down the hall and looked around for the office of the man he'd gone through BUD/S with years ago.

Life in the military was funny sometimes, because no matter what base he was headed to, he or one of the other guys already had a contact there. Matthew had made a call to an old friend and simple as that, he had a ride home from Pensacola. They'd drop Evan off at a hotel and then Matthew would face the music, returning to his childhood home. It wasn't even his own parents he had qualms about seeing, just his buddy Beckett's. Who happened to live right next door.

Evan caught up to him in the hall. "So you went through basic with this guy Colton?"

Matthew nodded. "Affirmative. We've kept in touch over the years. He's doing a one-year tour here in Pensacola, but normally he's an explosives guy."

"Yeah. Kind of figured with the name 'C-4'," Evan laughed.

Matthew smirked and knocked on the door of the office of Colton "C-4" Ferguson, clutching his duffle bag. It probably would've been easier catching a cab—then there'd be no need to explain to his old buddy what he was doing here in Pensacola. No reminder of his wounded friend.

But damn.

The sooner they got this show on the road, the sooner this weekend could be over. He didn't know if he could stomach seeing his best buddy injured. And what the hell kind of a friend did that make him anyway? He should be damn glad Beckett was alive, not feeling guilty for the things he could do that his friend would never be able to again. The sooner he faced Beckett and their new reality, the sooner Matthew could move forward with his life. Pretend this shit storm never happened.

With his SEAL team he had a mission, a purpose. But back home, when his best friend would be arriving in a wheelchair, missing one limb? No matter how hard he fought, how strong he was, nothing could change the past. Nothing could erase Beckett's injury. And for the first time ever, Matthew felt completely helpless.

# Chapter 2

Brianna Miller peeled off the sexy cocktail waitress dress she was wearing and pulled on a pair of cut-off denim shorts and soft cotton tank top. The low-cut dress with a short frilly skirt was the exact opposite of her style, and she wouldn't be caught dead in it outside of the bar where she worked. She stuffed the satiny black material into her oversized purse. The sooner she could burn it, the better.

The bar had no shortage of clientele on a Friday afternoon, she thought with a snort. Imagine that, men with plenty of money drinking too much and hitting on the pretty waitresses. Not exactly how she'd envisioned life after getting her MBA, but with lay-offs at the company she'd worked for and massive student loans to pay off, this was the best she could do. She was already living back at home with her parents at the age of twenty-six, as if that wasn't embarrassing enough.

She pulled her long blonde hair up into a loose bun and gathered the rest of her things. Surprise, surprise, the more makeup she wore and the more her straight, satiny hair swung around as she walked, the bigger the tips. Might as well work it, she thought. As degrading as that was.

Her friend Ella shot her a sideways glance from the adjoining locker. Her chocolate brown hair was piled high atop her head and her bright blue eyes could've brought many men to their knees. It actually had today, Brianna recalled with a grin, thinking of the drunk man who'd gotten down on bended knee and proposed to Ella before her shift ended. The ring he'd fashioned out of a strip of napkin hadn't exactly been what happily-ever-afters were made of, but the expression on his buddies' faces had made the whole thing worth it.

"What's so funny?" Ella asked, cocking her head.

"Just recalling your proposal tonight," Brianna said.

Ella rolled her eyes. "Ugh. Well, I guess it was better than some of things other customers have propositioned."

"Don't remind me," Brianna groaned.

Ella was a few years younger than Brianna and still working her way through college. While some of the other waitresses who worked here had no other aspirations, Brianna and Ella had quickly bonded over their desire to make a decent salary running cocktails for the filthy rich clientele and then move on with their lives. As quickly as possible.

"Do you have a shift tomorrow?" Ella asked.

"Unfortunately, yes," Brianna muttered.

"If you want the day off, just take it. It's your

brother's homecoming. I mean for God's sake, he was practically killed."

"I have off Sunday, plus next weekend to help him get settled in. I need this job, Ella. I've got massive student loan payments. I already got laid off from my real job, and that was supposed to pay for my MBA."

"Smarty pants," Ella teased, sticking her tongue out at Brianna.

"Right. All those years of school and I can't even get a good job in this crappy market."

Ella shrugged. "So move. There're jobs out there somewhere."

"Maybe. But now's not the time. My parents need me with everything that's happened with Beckett. He needs me. Maybe in a year or so if nothing changes I'll expand my scope, but I'm sure I'll find a decent job before then."

"This isn't decent?" Ella asked with a smirk. Her eyes flashed with amusement, and for the millionth time, Brianna was grateful she had her. There was no way she'd survive day after day in this job otherwise. Her friends from business school were all off working their way up the corporate ladder. Her parents didn't know she'd lost her lucrative marketing job. The only person she'd confessed to was Beckett, and he was madder than hell at her for taking this job as a cocktail waitress. But there'd been little he could do about it when he was a million miles away on the other side of the world. Now that he was home, however, was a different story. She'd led him to believe that she'd moved on to something else, but with him injured, now wasn't exactly the time to fess up.

Brianna slammed her locker shut. They'd given her

Sunday off, the day of her brother's arrival from Walter Reed. But since she'd told her manager she needed next weekend off to help him, they'd put her on the schedule today and tomorrow. As if she needed creepy, drunk men trying to slip their hands up her skirt. It was bad enough to deal with that on an average day, but when her world had been turned upside down at the sudden near-fatal injury of her brother? Those assholes she served drinks to were lucky she hadn't dumped a cocktail right over their heads. And followed it up by a good slap in the face or knee to the groin. Because that wouldn't get her fired or anything.

"I'll see you tomorrow?" she asked, glancing back at Ella.

"I'll be here, same as always. And tonight I'll be drowning in a term paper. You know you're lucky to already have two degrees, right?"

"Plus, don't forget I have all this," Brianna said, twirling her finger around as she smiled in a brief moment of levity. Despite the grief and shock she'd gone through over the past month, she could count on Ella to cheer her up. Brianna might not have a career or her own place at the moment, but friendship counted for something. And she needed that more than ever right now.

She walked out to the parking lot, tossing her purse onto the passenger seat of her convertible. Geez. If she didn't find a high-paying job in the marketing field soon, she might have to sell her baby and get something less expensive. She sighed. As if she needed another problem to worry about at the moment.

Brianna started the engine, switched on the radio,

and backed out of her parking space. A group of men climbing out of a BMW a few spaces down whistled appreciatively at her as she pulled away.

*Good grief.*

She'd gone to college and business school just to prance around in a skimpy outfit all day serving drinks? Un-freaking-believable.

She pushed the speed dial for Beckett's number as she cruised down the road. He had physical therapy sessions on Friday afternoons, but hopefully she could catch him when he was back in his room.

"Hey little sis," he answered as way of greeting. His voice sounded strained, and worry creased her brow.

"Are you okay?"

"Yeah, just wiped out. My entire body hurts at the moment."

"It's good for you to exercise. Are you all set to fly down here on Sunday?"

"Yeah, I'm about ready to bust out of this joint. I'm not sure how I'll manage getting around on one leg, but the doctors assure me I'll adjust. It sucks to be a Navy SEAL who can barely even dress himself in the morning, but one of these days I hope to be up and about again."

"You will," Brianna assured him, feeling uncertainty creep into her chest. He had to. She couldn't imagine her fearless brother needing to depend on anyone. As much as it pained her, it had to be about a million times worse for him.

"I'm not sure if I can take much more of this hospital food," he admitted. "So it will be good to get out of here. I just don't want to be a burden to Mom and Dad."

"You're not a burden," Brianna protested. "Plus don't forget I moved back home. I'll be there to help out."

"I'm thirty years old, Brianna. I shouldn't have to depend on my parents or little sister."

"We're family. Of course we'll help you. Wouldn't you help me if the situation was reversed?"

"That's not the same thing," Beckett argued.

"Why not?"

"Because I'm a man. A God damn Navy SEAL. I'm used to being the guy to get things done when no one else can. Taking on dangerous operations. But not being able to move around my own house without assistance? That just isn't right."

"It's not forever," Brianna assured him softly. "I mean, you'll adjust to your new life."

"I don't know," he said grimly. "I've been here over a month and feel like I don't have a damn thing to show for it."

"We can talk Sunday if you want. I just got to the grocery store—I'm picking up things for your big homecoming party."

"Yeah, the party," he muttered. "I'm not sure if I'm in the mood to deal with a house full of guests."

"But Mom and Dad are so excited you're coming home."

"Yeah, yeah. What are you doing off on Friday afternoon anyhow? You haven't found a new job yet?"

Brianna paled, and was relieved they were talking over the phone and not in person. Otherwise her brother would certainly see right through her. "I'm still looking," she said lightly. "I sent out a bunch of resumes this week."

"Good," he said.

Beckett didn't say anything about the job he thought she'd quit at the cocktail lounge. It was just as well. She didn't want to get into it with him, and he had enough on his plate as it was. Getting readjusted to civilian life and to life with only one leg would be hard on anyone. He would do it, but he sure didn't need to deal with her problems as well. She was going to turn her life back around pronto. Just as soon as she got through the next week.

\*\*\*

Matthew narrowed his eyes in the passenger seat as Colton pulled into his parents' driveway. The same house he'd grown up in greeted him, complete with a two-car garage, neat landscaping, and his mother's potted plants and colorful flowers on the front porch. But that's not what his gaze was drawn to.

A shiny new Mustang convertible was parked in the driveway next door at Beckett's house. And at the moment, a hotter than hell blonde was leaning over the trunk, pulling out bags of groceries. The skimpy little denim shorts she had on did little to conceal her miles of tanned, toned legs and perfectly highlighted her heart-shaped ass. His dick immediately jerked to attention, and Matthew clenched his teeth. He was home to attend his buddy's homecoming ceremony. Not to feast eyes on the pretty little thing that had pulled up in Beckett's driveway. Was that his…girlfriend? Surely Beckett would have mentioned if he was dating someone. And if she was, she'd be with him at Walter Reed. Maybe she was some relative he'd never met? Like a cousin or something?

Matthew opened the car door and nodded at Colton. "Thanks again for the lift, man. And for dropping Evan off at his hotel."

"No problem. It was the least I could do. I'm sorry about your buddy, but I'll be there at the arrival ceremony on Sunday."

"Thanks. Are you working tomorrow afternoon? We'll be back on base to pick up some SEAL buddies of mine who're flying in for the ceremony."

"Probably so. Stop by my office before you head out. We can all grab a drink."

"Damn straight," Matthew agreed, shutting the passenger door and then reaching into the backseat to grab his duffle bag. He nodded again at Colton as their eyes met in the rearview mirror and then stepped back, taking a deep breath as he steeled himself to go inside.

Usually coming home felt good, but this time, it was for all the wrong reasons. Seeing the pain on his parents' faces over the injury of the man they'd thought of as a second son would be gut-wrenching. And eventually seeing Beckett's parents? Brutal. He had half a mind to turn around and catch the next flight back to Virginia.

He was a SEAL used to going into battle, getting sent on missions all over the world, charging at armed insurgents. But he couldn't stand the thought of facing his best friend's parents? What kind of asshole was he? His buddy was injured, not dead. He needed to man the hell up and face whatever came his way.

The trunk slammed in the driveway next door, and he resisted the urge to look over. Why the hell tempt himself with something he couldn't have? He'd be here and gone again, just like that. There were plenty of pretty women back home in Virginia. No sense in getting mixed up with Beckett's friend or relative or whoever the hell the goddess next door turned out to be.

"Matthew?"

A voice sweeter than honey called out his name, and he blinked behind his aviators, momentarily dazed. How in the hell did the gorgeous blonde know his name?

Turning around, he saw that the woman he'd been ogling was now watching him suspiciously. Confusion knit her brows, but those pouty pink lips were open in surprise. Straight, almost white-blonde hair hung to her breasts, which looked supple and tempting beneath the yellow tank top she wore. The top was loosely tucked into her shorts, which hung from her curvy hips in a way that was positively dangerous.

She was way too enticing. The kind of woman that a man wanted to kiss all over and pleasure all night. He was dying to peel off that clingy top and tug down those sexier-than-sin little shorts. What did she have on beneath those tiny little scraps of denim? A bikini? Thong? Satin or lace? He was practically salivating to find out. And hell if that was the very last thing he should be after right now.

"Matthew, right?" she asked again, cocking her head. She pursed her pretty lips together, watching him.

*Hell.*

The thought of those full lips wrapped around his cock had him instantly hard again. Pink gloss coated them, although she wore more makeup than the women he usually went after. But she was gorgeous. Would be even without all that stuff caked on. And she had a killer body he'd love to explore, he thought as his gaze swept over her again from head to toe. Every single inch of.

What the hell was wrong with him?

He was here for his buddy, not to chase after women. Especially one that was apparently staying right next door. That was a friend or relative of Beckett's. She sure the hell wasn't the next chick he was going to take to bed.

Matthew cleared his throat. "Yes, that's right. I'm Matthew. Do we know each other, darlin'?"

*Where the fuck had that come from?*

Yes, it looked like he was flirting. Right here. Right now. Two days before his buddy returned home missing one limb.

"You don't recognize me," she said with a small smile. He felt a strange tightening in his chest. Hell, he'd do anything to erase that look off her face, but since she was parked in Beckett's driveway, she had to be upset for the same damn reason he was. His injured friend. The homecoming ceremony. It sure the hell had nothing to do with him.

He took a step closer, dropping his duffle bag to the ground. His heart did a funny little stutter, like it knew something his brain didn't, and blood pounded through his veins. All the air felt like it had been sucked from his lungs, and he couldn't for the life of him figure out whether to move closer or retreat. Her wide sea green eyes stared at him, now somewhat amused. His mind was desperately trying to play catch up with his body, which was reacting to her on a primal level. To kiss her. Touch her. Claim her.

Make her his.

But what the hell was that about? He hit on pretty

women all the time. Went to bed with them even more often. What made her so damn appealing? He was missing something here, and as a trained SEAL, that didn't sit well with him.

The image of a little girl in pigtails suddenly sprung into his mind, of endless summers exploring the great outdoors and a trio of inseparable kids. His gut twisted even as his pulse raced. This wasn't some sexy as hell woman he didn't know. Not some long lost relative of Beckett's that he could hope to coax into bed as a distraction from the current hell he was living. Not some pretty blonde he could enjoy the weekend with and then never see again.

"It's me," she finally said. "Brianna."

Nope, this was FUBAR—fucked up beyond all recognition. He was lusting over his best friend's little sister.

# Chapter 3

Matthew's jaw dropped, and Brianna knew he really hadn't recognized her. It had been what? Maybe ten years since she'd last seen him? Beckett and Matthew had enlisted in the military right after they'd graduated from high school. She'd just finished eighth grade, ready to move onto high school, and they were ready to see the whole damn world. Leaving her behind.

She'd trailed after them all through childhood, and they hadn't seemed to mind having her along on their adventures. It wasn't until the tender age of thirteen, when Matthew was seventeen, that she'd started to see him as something other than her older brother's best friend. Something more special than just the boy next door.

Not that he'd paid her any special attention. He'd been tall and handsome even then—attracting all the high school girls and some of the pretty college co-eds that were around for Pensacola's beaches with his tall physique, tanned muscles, and bright green eyes.

And as for today? Holy hell.

He'd filled out in ways she could never have imagined when she was younger, with muscles bulging from beneath the arms of the short-sleeved polo shirt he wore, jeans that hung perfectly from his narrow hips, and a wide chest that she longed to sink into.

Just imagining those massive arms wrapped around her, those muscular hands trailing over her skin, had her heart rate palpitating and desire pooling at her core. She'd been attracted to him when she was younger, yes—in a school girlish sort of way. In wanting him to pull her aside and steal a kiss.

But now? Damn. She wanted a whole night in his arms—surrounded by his strength. She wanted the weight of his muscular body atop hers, the feel of his lips against her own, and his throbbing manhood buried deep inside her swollen flesh.

She blushed, trying to shake the image she had of them tangled up in the sheets together. She'd only had one serious relationship, and it had been far from satisfying. Something about the way Matthew carried himself let her know that she would know exactly how to please a woman. And something about the way her body always responded to him let her know a night with him wouldn't disappoint. But who was she kidding? He was her older brother's best friend. He'd never seen her as anything other than the girl next door, and even if they were both adults now, perfectly capable of making their own decisions, he'd never make a move on Beckett's little sister.

She blew out a sigh as Matthew finally regained his wits and walked over to her. She was about to hold her hand out in greeting when he suddenly engulfed her in a hug. His muscular arms wrapped around her, his chest pressing against her breasts as he pulled her close. His chin rested atop her head, his entire body surrounding hers. He was solid as a rock but warm. It shouldn't have felt so damn good to have him hold her, but she unwittingly melted into his firm embrace. Her cheek fell against the thick cotton of his polo shirt, and his scent surrounded her—soap, mixed in with a muskiness that was all Matthew.

"Holy hell, Brianna, I didn't even recognize you," he said gruffly. He released her all too quickly, and she stepped back, tilting her head up to meet his gaze. Slight stubble coated his strong jaw, but it was those green eyes that did her in. It was like they could see right into her soul.

"It hasn't been that long, has it?" she asked lightly.

"Damn near ten years," Matthew chuckled, crossing his arms casually. "You've grown up." She took in the corded muscles of his forearms, the veins bulging from those strong hands. Hell. He wasn't just the guy next door anymore. He was a Navy SEAL now—a warrior. He'd been around the world. Seen things she'd never dreamed of. Been with more women than she could probably ever count.

"Ten years is a long time," she said softly, regret winding through her. "I'd say we've all changed."

"The last time I saw you was sometime when I was home on leave. You were still in high school and dating that goofy kid from down the street as I recall."

Brianna blushed, remembering her brother and Matthew watching as she left on a date one night. They'd both seemed amused, and the poor guy she was with had seemed terrified. "How on Earth could you remember that?"

Matthew winked. "I didn't like him hanging around you."

Unexpected warmth seeped through her. He was just being a protective older brother type. It certainly didn't mean anything. Brianna shrugged, feeling like a teenager all over again, and she didn't miss the way Matthew's gaze slid to her chest.

*Hmmm.*

"Well, anyway, he was harmless. And I'm single now."

Matthew raised his eyebrows, a smile playing about his lips.

*Crap. Why on Earth had she said that?*

"I'm surprised," he said with an easy grin. "Especially without Beckett and me here to chase all the guys away." He cleared his throat, his eyes clouding at the mention of Beckett.

"I went up to visit him at Walter Reed," Brianna said, suddenly feeling uncomfortable. "It was bad, really bad."

Matthew nodded grimly.

"It was good of you to come this weekend. He'll need the support. I talked to him earlier, and he seemed pretty down in the dumps about coming home and needing our help."

Matthew chuffed out a laugh. "That's Beckett. Too damn stubborn to let anyone help him with anything. Too damn stubborn to die, I suppose."

Brianna nodded grimly. "Some of the other guys he was with didn't make it. The Navy wouldn't tell us any of the details, but Beckett told me they're gone."

"I should've gone up to see him," Matthew said,

looking pained. "It's only a couple of hours from Little Creek. I could've taken leave or driven up one weekend…."

Brianna reached out and touched his tanned forearm, and Matthew flinched. His eyes met hers. "He was really out of it, Matthew. He wouldn't even have remembered that you were there. It's better that you came now. I don't think he would've wanted you to see him that way. Not like that."

He nodded, swallowing, and Brianna slowly pulled her hand back, instantly missing the warmth of his skin beneath her fingertips. The solid strength of him. She glanced over to the groceries she'd left on the ground behind her car. "Anyway, I better get those inside before everything melts in this heat. My parents are out picking up things for Sunday, and I swung by the grocery store…."

"I'll help you," Matthew said, striding over to the back of her car.

She followed, coming to a stop next to him. His large frame loomed over her, and she tried to ignore the way her pulse pounded as his arm brushed against hers. He had pounds of muscle beneath all that tanned skin, and the thought of all that strength inside of her was terrifying. Exhilarating.

The idea of Matthew making love to her set every last nerve ending on fire, and heat washed over her skin. She'd never be with Matthew in that way. She'd never even kiss him. So why her mind was conjuring up images of Matthew's powerful body atop hers, she'd never know.

Brianna grabbed the last bag, amused that Matthew was holding the other four. Was he showing off for her? Or just being a southern gentleman?

Walking over to the passenger side of her car, she grabbed her oversized purse from the seat, making sure her uniform was completely stuffed inside it, and headed toward the front door. Matthew was hot on her heels, and she added an extra little swing to her step. She thought she heard him mutter something under his breath and grinned.

Matthew cleared his throat. "Sweet ride," he said, trailing behind her. She glanced over her shoulder to see him looking back at her car. And was it her imagination, or was there a slight bulge in his pants that hadn't been there before?

"Thanks. I just bought it last year."

"So last I heard," Matthew continued, "you have some fancy marketing job? You always were the smart one in the family."

Brianna inwardly cringed. It was doubtful that she'd see Matthew again after this weekend, so why bore him with news of her layoff and current less-than-desirable job situation? There was no way she was telling him the embarrassing truth. That yes, she had her MBA, but she'd lost her job and was currently collecting tips as a cocktail waitress. A job she didn't need any type of degree for. "Uh, yeah," she agreed. "I've been in marketing for two years."

*There. Not a total lie.*

"No kidding. And you moved back in with your folks?"

She shrugged, feeling herself flush. "Beckett could use the help while he recovers. And it's not forever."

She pulled her keys from her purse and fidgeted with the lock, her whole body pulsing with awareness as Matthew came to a stop right behind her. Goose bumps coated her skin despite the heat, and she felt even more attuned to him now than when he'd briefly embraced her moments ago. Heat radiated off his large frame as she stood between him and the door, and she could still smell the musky scent of his skin. He was so close and so far all at the same time. Confusion wrapped around her mind.

Finally, she got the front door open, hoping he didn't notice how long it had taken. Or why she'd been so distracted. Feeling flustered, she gestured for him to go ahead while she closed the door.

The familiar scent of her parents' home filled the air—the slight trace of the lemon cleaner her mom always used, the lingering scent of the muffins her mom had made at breakfast that morning. Framed photographs lined the walls of the hallway, and she tried not to cringe as she spotted the one of her, Beckett, and Matthew as kids. Her brother looked so happy and carefree in it. Would she ever see him smile like that again?

They carried the groceries into the kitchen, and Matthew hefted the four bags he was carrying onto the counter as if they weighed nothing at all. She watched his shirt stretch across his muscular back, and her eyes slid lower to his narrow hips. He looked powerful and domineering yet perfectly at ease in her kitchen. She quickly looked away before he caught her watching him. So what if he looked like some sort of statue of a bronze god come to life? She had no business wanting him that way. Or in any way.

"Looks just like I remember it," Matthew said, a smile coming to his face as he glanced around the cozy kitchen.

"Yeah, Mom and Dad haven't changed much over the years. Just like old times…." Her voice trailed off as she thought how nothing would be like "old times" again. Not with Beckett missing a leg, getting around in a wheelchair. Not when her older brother, the big, bad Navy SEAL would never be sent on an op with his team again. She'd grown used to not knowing where he was, but to know he was stuck sitting at their parents' house in a wheelchair? She wasn't sure which scenario was more gut-wrenching.

"How is Beckett now?" Matthew asked, evidently thinking the same thing as her. "Seriously. My folks haven't told me everything—I'm sure of that. Mom didn't want me to worry while I was deployed with the team."

Brianna blew out a sigh. "Down in the dumps. Lucky to be alive. Upset that his career as a Navy SEAL is over."

Matthew nodded, his jaw tightening. It had to be hard for him, Brianna realized. Beckett and Matthew did everything together, from the time they were kids right up until they graduated from high school and enlisted in the Navy. She doubted many men became SEALs, but somehow they both did. And they were damn good at their jobs. Now Matthew would continue his career and Beckett would be sidelined at a desk job. No matter what, from this point forward, things would never be the same again.

Brianna pulled a gallon of milk from one of the grocery bags, trying to distract herself from the unwanted memories, and Matthew relieved her of it instantly, his fingertips brushing against hers. "I got it," he said, his voice gruff.

His biceps bulged as he easily lifted it away, and she tried not to stare at the massive man in front of her. The walls of muscles spanning his chest were impressive. Intimidating. Inviting. She wanted to skim over them with her fingertips, exploring each dip and ridge. To smooth her palms over his broad pectorals. To kiss her way over this man, learning about the hardened warrior he'd become over their years apart. Which was completely crazy. The spark she'd felt as his fingers brushed against hers was ridiculous. It certainly shouldn't have sent warmth seeping through her entire body. Or made her breath catch and nipples tighten.

She abruptly turned away, taking a deep breath as she grabbed some more items from the bags. At least she'd been grocery shopping and not out buying tampons or something. Matthew probably would've insisted on helping carry her bags inside then, too. Groceries, she could handle at least. Walking purposefully across the kitchen, she opened one of the cupboards, stretching up onto her tiptoes to shove the boxes of pasta up onto a high shelf.

She heard the fridge door slam shut, and when she turned back around she found that Matthew was watching her, his eyes molten.

He'd gone completely still, seeming unsure whether to bolt from the room or cross it, collecting her in his arms. She met his gaze, and the warmth coiling in her belly snaked down to her core. She wondered what it would be like to kiss Matthew. To taste him. To let him hold her just for one night.

Crazily enough, she was certain that a night with Matthew in her bed would be better than a thousand nights with another man. She'd been in love with him forever—first in a silly, school girlish way, and then in the way that you start to care for someone you've known forever. There was lust there, yes, but she was certain she'd also been in love with him all this time.

When she'd heard from Beckett years ago that Matthew had returned from his first deployment, it had been gut-wrenching. She'd never know where he was, when he'd return, or if he was safe. Scratch that—he was likely always in danger when he deployed. And just like that, the boy next door had turned into a man with a life and career of his own— one that would never include her.

Their eyes locked for a second more, some unspoken bond tethering them together, and then Matthew cleared his throat, breaking the spell. "I should go. I just got in, and I haven't even seen my folks yet."

Brianna shakily nodded in agreement. He should definitely go. Before either one of them did something foolish. Before she blurted out something she'd always regret.

"Thanks for your help," she said softly. "Can I get you a drink or something before you leave?"

He nodded, his eyes burning. "A glass of water would be great," he said, his voice gravel.

She silently moved to another cupboard, pulling out two glasses. When she turned back around Matthew was already right there behind her, and she gasped. She hadn't even heard him move across the room. A beat passed before Matthew took both glasses from her and crossed to the fridge, filling each glass with ice and water.

"I didn't even ask what you wanted to drink," he said as he handed her one of the cups.

"Water's perfect." She took a sip, the cool liquid seeping down her throat, and suddenly felt like the entire room was too hot.

Or maybe it was just the man standing in front of her.

Matthew drained his water in one long gulp. His eyes were softer as he gazed at her once more, and briefly, he skimmed his thumb across her cheek. "It was good to see you Brianna."

She froze, too startled by his caress to say anything else.

"I'll see you Sunday."

His abrupt dismissal felt like a dagger to her chest. Of course she wouldn't see him again until Sunday. He was here for Beckett's homecoming, not to catch up on old times with her. Not to spend Friday night reminiscing about their younger years. They barely even knew each other anymore. Not really. And that moment that had just passed between them was just that—a moment. Fleeting. Ephemeral. Probably already forgotten by him.

"Right, I'll see you then," she said tightly, turning back to put away the rest of the groceries. She heard Matthew's quiet footsteps as he retreated back toward the front door, and then she was alone, surrounded by nothing but deafening silence.

\*\*\*

Matthew released a breath he didn't even know he'd been holding as he crossed the lawn back to his parents' house. What the hell had just happened? His pulse pounded as he tried to get a grip. He clenched his firsts, grinding his jaw, and snatched up the duffle bag he'd left in their driveway. He needed to go for a ten-mile run to let out his pent-up sexual frustration, or if nothing else, take a very, very cold shower.

Because the hard-on he'd been sporting since he'd first seen Brianna bending over the trunk of her car?

*Holy hell.*

He had no damn business looking at the girl—woman—who'd always been like a kid sister to him like that. He had no right to want her that way. But when he'd followed her inside, inhaling her light floral scent, watching that long blonde hair swish back and forth? He'd been a goner. Then she'd turned away from him, stretching up on those toned legs to reach the top shelf?

*Jesus.*

Her gorgeous legs went on for miles, leading up to that sweet ass he'd very much like to palm as he pulled her closer. Her lithe body was tanned, toned, and curvy in all the right places. Soft exactly where he was hard.

He'd longed to cross the kitchen, pull her into his arms, and kiss her. Just to see how she'd react. And hell, who was he kidding? What he'd really wanted to do was bend her over the counter, palm those lush breasts, and sink his way straight into heaven. The idea of their bodies joined together with her crying out his name in pleasure would be something he'd never forget.

Hell, she was a woman now, only four years younger than him. Not the girl who'd trailed after Beckett and him as kids. But something about her was still innocent and pure. Not like the bold women who came onto him and his buddies back home. Who flaunted their bodies and practically begged to be taken home for the night. And hell if he didn't want to spend time getting fully reacquainted with Brianna. Intimately.

He counted to ten, willing his body to calm down before he went inside his childhood home. It was ridiculous to even consider the notion of having Brianna that way—like she was his every fantasy come to life. Like he'd really fuck a woman he cared about, felt protective toward, in the middle of her kitchen after not seeing her in years.

Like his best friend wouldn't bust his ass for even thinking about it.

*Shit.*

He gulped down air as the guilt threatened to overtake him. It wasn't his fault Beckett was injured. Not really. Even if he hadn't convinced him to enlist a lifetime ago, Beckett probably damn would've done so anyway. Just to keep up with Matthew. Just because he was that damn stubborn.

They were childhood friends, yes, but now brothers in arms.

He needed to man the hell up and be there for his buddy. His brother. To face their families as they dealt with the new reality and stay the hell away from his sister.

Finally, he pushed open the front door, shaking his head at the fact that it was unlocked. His parents didn't have a worry in the world, but he'd have to talk to them about at least locking up the house. He certainly wasn't around to protect them if necessary, and hell. You never knew who could walk right in here. He'd even made sure Brianna's door was secured before he pulled it shut behind him when he left. Regretfully. Because wouldn't he love to go back over there and see what it was simmering between them. Hell, they'd only been in each other's presence for ten minutes. And for him to be this riled up over that? A night with her in his arms would be fucking spectacular.

But that was the crux of it, wasn't it? Because one night with her would never be enough. And she deserved far better than a one-night-stand with her older brother's best friend.

"Matthew, is that you?" his mom called from the kitchen.

He muttered a curse under his breath. If she left the damn door unlocked, it could be just about anyone, now couldn't it?

"Yeah, it's me."

She came rushing into the room, embracing him in a hug. "Thank goodness you made it home safely! Beckett's parents have been so upset since his accident. I'm always so worried about you doing your SEAL stuff. But I know they'll be so happy to see you—Beckett, too."

"I'm fine, Mom."

"Your job is just so dangerous…," she trailed off, fretting.

"We're well trained. And although accidents can happen, that's the risk you take when you join the military. Beckett knew it, and so did I." His voice sounded harsher than he'd intended, but hell. The guilt was practically eating him alive.

"Have you seen his parents? Oh, what am I saying, you just got home. Of course you haven't seen anyone yet."

Matthew resisted the urge to smile. His mother always fawned over him when he happened to get leave to make it home. That was the crux of being an only child. Some things never changed.

She pulled back, appraising him with green eyes so

similar to his. "Did you eat yet? I could fix you something."

"I grabbed lunch earlier before my flight. Think I'll go for a run after I get settled in."

"Did you friend come down? Evan, was it?"

"Yeah, but he's staying at a hotel. He knows Beckett and has some other friends in town he wanted to catch up with. You'll meet him on Sunday at the homecoming ceremony. Some of my other buddies may come in then as well."

"He's welcome to stay here, you know."

"I'm sure he's cool with the hotel. Did you need help with anything before I go for a run?"

"No, no. Everything's fine. Just be sure to wash up in time for dinner. Your father will be home around six. He's out running some errands now."

"Roger that, ma'am."

His mom playfully swatted his arm and disappeared back into the kitchen. Briefly, images of Brianna moving around her kitchen flashed through his mind. Hell, carrying in groceries for her earlier and watching her put things away felt like the most natural thing the world. What would it be like having her fixing him dinner, looking forward to his return home? How would it feel to come home to someone like her every night?

Hell. What was he thinking? She had her MBA and some sort of hot-shot marketing career. She was on the fast-track to success. She wouldn't want to take care of a man—or to let a man take care of her.

Nope, he was better off alone, just as he'd always been.

Matthew glanced at his watch—Becket would be arriving in less than forty-eight hours. Two days here, and he could fly back to Little Creek and forget the whole clusterfuck of seeing his best friend injured. Of pretending things would ever be the same again. Of trying to convince himself that Brianna was just the girl next door and not someone who could actually make him imagine a future with a woman. Only question was, how was he supposed to get through the weekend until then?

.

# Chapter 4

"I invited the Murphys over for dessert tonight," Brianna's mother said as they loaded the dishwasher after dinner. "Did you know Matthew's back already?"

Brianna nearly dropped the plate she was holding. "What? Why?"

"Brianna," her mother admonished. "What's the matter with you? We haven't seen Matthew in years, and he's one of Beckett's best friends."

"No, I mean why did you invite them over? We'll see them on Sunday with everyone else." Heat washed over her skin as she recalled Matthew moving around the kitchen earlier. Looking like he belonged there or something. And the way he'd brushed his thumb across her cheek before he left? She knew she hadn't imagined the heat in his eyes. The spark of interest that he'd had in that moment.

But the entire thing was completely ridiculous—he

wasn't interested in her that way. She was acting like a schoolgirl with a crush on the captain of the football team or something. She was a grown woman for heaven's sake. If her parents wanted to invite the neighbors over, then so be it. Maybe she should say she'd already made plans for the evening. Then she could be polite but keep her distance from Matthew when she saw him again on Sunday.

How was she supposed to act natural with him sitting here in the same room as her? The attraction she'd felt for him years ago had only bloomed in their time spent apart. He wasn't a teenage boy anymore but a grown man. A Navy SEAL who had traveled the world. And since he'd be gone again in a matter of days, there was no point in imagining anything happening between them. Not now and not ever.

"They've been nothing but supportive with everything we've been dealing with as far as Beckett's recovery is concerned. Plus your father ran into Mr. Murphy while he was out running errands earlier. He mentioned Matthew was back, and we thought you kids would enjoy seeing one another."

Brianna laughed. "Mom, I'm twenty-six. Matthew is thirty. We're not exactly kids anymore. And we actually ran into each other this afternoon. If we wanted to see each other tonight, we could've made plans." She picked up her glass from the counter and took a sip.

"I think Matthew's mom would like to see him settled down. You know, she always hoped you two would end up together."

Brianna nearly spit out her water. "Excuse me?"

"Matthew's her only son. And she's always loved you like a daughter."

"I'm pretty sure Matthew only sees me as a kid sister type. I trailed after him and Beckett for years, and when they left, I'm almost positive he forgot all about me."

Her mother laughed. "Well that's not true at all. He always asked about you when he was back in town. More so than Beckett even," her mom added with a chuckle.

Brianna raised her eyebrows. Matthew had been checking up on her all this time? She thought the guy had practically vanished off the face of the Earth. Funny that this was the first time her mom had mentioned it—now that she had temporarily moved back home and Matthew was conveniently right next door. "What time are they coming by?"

"Eight."

She glanced down at the cut-offs and tank top she still had on as the feeling of butterflies took hold in her stomach. "Thanks for all the notice."

\*\*\*

Matthew rang the doorbell of Beckett's house that evening, his parents standing behind him. He didn't know how he'd gotten roped into having dessert with the neighbors tonight, but this was exactly the sort of interaction he was trying to avoid. He couldn't bear looking into their eyes as they saw him, healthy with two legs, while his best friend was still in a hospital. That shit just wasn't fair, and he'd hoped to see his buddy on Sunday, show his support, and make a hasty departure. But facing his friend's parents, who were practically like a second family to him? That shit was brutal.

Not to mention having to spend the evening with Brianna. Holy hell. He'd taken a cold shower before and after his run earlier. That's how worked up he was from ten minutes together. Since when had the girl he'd always known turned into such a smoking hot woman? He'd kept tabs on her over the years—asking Beckett or his parents how she was doing. Watching from afar when she was younger and still in school when he happened to be in town. But the years had slipped way, and she sure the hell wasn't some school girl anymore. She was all woman—with curves to tempt and tease him, long blonde hair he'd love to run his fingers through, and skin so luscious he wanted to explore every inch of it.

She was the total package—all wrapped up in his buddy's kid sister. So what if she wasn't a kid anymore; a guy didn't go after his best friend's sister. No matter how gorgeous she was. And hell—he'd been practically like a second older brother all these years. It was a damn bad idea, plain and simple. Maybe he could make a hasty departure, feigning exhaustion from his travels. Maybe—

Brianna opened the door a moment later, pushing all those thoughts from his mind, and Matthew had to remind himself how to breathe.

Her soft blonde hair fell past her shoulders, the tips of it just kissing her breasts. She had on a soft blouse and dark jeans, but hell. She might as well have been wearing nothing at all from the way his groin tightened and pulse pounded. The soft fabric of her top pulled across her full breasts, and those jeans looked like they'd practically been painted on with the way her killer curves were on display. Even though she was wearing more clothing than when he'd seen her earlier, she looked sexier than ever.

*She's Beckett's little sister. She's Beckett's little sister.*

Maybe if he told himself that a thousand times, his body would catch up with his brain. But right now, his cock was rock-hard and his libido was roaring. He shifted uncomfortably on the front porch.

"Hi Matthew, Mr. and Mrs. Murphy," Brianna said brightly, completely oblivious to his distress. She gestured for them to come inside. "Thanks for coming over."

Matthew walked in first, Brianna's floral scent surrounding him. Was that perfume? Her shampoo? It was so sweet and innocent that he had the craziest urge to wrap her up in his arms and never let her go. Which was completely bat shit crazy. Hell, what would the other dudes on his team think of him acting this way about a woman? It was true that four of the guys were now happily in relationships, but as for Matthew? Not a chance in hell. He was more a love 'em and leave 'em type. And he made sure the women he took home always knew the score.

Not that he'd be getting any action this weekend staying with his folks. Tonight was family night, tomorrow he'd go out with the guys, and Sunday would be all about Beckett. So certainly he could keep a certain female off his mind for the next forty-eight hours. Too bad he was currently standing in her living room.

Matthew's mom followed him in, hugging Brianna's parents. "We just can't wait to see Beckett on Sunday. Is he excited to finally be coming home? It must be such a relief to know he'll be here in a matter of days."

After the Millers tearfully greeted Matthew, the

two mothers settled in to chat on the sofa while Brianna's dad went to get them drinks. Soon Matthew was left standing alone with Brianna in the front hall, feeling as nervous as a dumb teenager. His eyes skimmed over her, from her blonde hair and sweet face, down over her womanly curves. She looked a hell of a lot better than she did earlier all done up in that makeup. More natural, but also about a thousand times more beautiful. He was such a goner.

"What?" she asked, looking up at him with wide eyes the color of the sea.

"You look nice," he finally said. Nice was the understatement of the century. Fucking spectacular would have been more appropriate. He cleared his throat. "So are we really going to sit around here while our parents chit-chat all night?"

Brianna laughed, a spark in her eyes. "What'd you have in mind?"

Matthew shrugged. Why the hell was he suddenly feeling tongue-tied around her? This girl probably knew him as well as he knew himself. He hardly had a childhood memory without her in it. "We could grab a drink, go for a walk, whatever. I just need to do something. Get out of here. Too many memories...."

Brianna smiled. "I'd love to get out of here. And luckily for you, I've got just the place in mind."

Ten minutes later, they were cruising down the road in Brianna's convertible. Matthew felt foolish letting a woman drive him around, but what was he supposed to do? It was either this or borrow one of his parents' cars like he was a high school kid again. And Brianna had actually laughed when he'd offered to drive her car.

"Where are we going, anyway?"

"This cute little bar down by the beach. It's new, but I think you'll love it. We can grab a drink and enjoy the sunset."

"Can't go wrong with that," Matthew agreed.

"So how long are you in town?" Brianna asked a few minutes later as she turned off the engine. Matthew was half-tempted to run around the car and open the door for her, but he wasn't the dating type of guy. And this sure the hell wasn't a date. Just two friends grabbing a drink. Nothing more.

*Right.*

Her car door slammed shut, and he resisted the urge to go to her, escorting her across the parking lot. Touching some of that soft skin. They were just friends. Not a damn thing had changed.

Brianna continued speaking as they walked toward the bar. "Maybe we could take Beckett out one night for a beer. Does that sound good?"

Matthew cleared his throat, feeling guilty. "Uh, I'm supposed to fly out Sunday night."

"Really?" Brianna paused at the door, turning to face him, and Matthew nearly bumped into her. Luckily he'd stopped just in time, or he'd be clutching her to him so she didn't fall over, those lush breasts of hers pressed up against his chest. Hell. Maybe he should've knocked the woman right over. Trapped her against the door with his body and kissed her thoroughly, just to see if their chemistry was only in his imagination.

Just to get her out of his system.

He ground his jaw, stepping around her to reach for the handle. "Yeah, I was lucky my CO gave me time off," Matthew said, pulling open the door and gesturing for Brianna to walk inside.

A few pairs of male eyes slid her way, and Matthew nearly draped his arm around her shoulders, pulling her close. Staking his claim. But what exactly would that prove? She wasn't his. Nevertheless, his chest tightened and his eyes narrowed as he glared at the group of dudes at the nearby table. They hastily went back to their drinks, and Matthew felt a certain sense of male pride building inside him.

Hell.

If he'd acted like any more of a caveman, he would've beaten his chest and hauled her over his shoulder, taking her away from other men's prying eyes. Taking her somewhere and proving that she was meant to be his.

He glanced back at Brianna, and his heart stuttered slightly as he caught the expression on her face.

"Right," she said, looking slightly forlorn. "Well, I'll take Beckett out for a beer sometime. Eventually. It'll just be hard with the wheelchair. He's still getting used to it of course. And I know he'd love to spend time catching up with you…."

Her voice trailed off, and Matthew suddenly wanted to do anything to take the sadness out of her eyes. This was exactly why he hadn't wanted to spend time with Beckett's family while he was here. Matthew couldn't stomach it. Seeing Beckett's parents in distress was hard enough earlier, but to see Brianna upset? He didn't think he could bear her tears.

She hastened a glance up at him, and Matthew could see moisture in her eyes. Holy hell. His chest clenched uncomfortably, and he watched as her lower lip trembled. Seeing her sad almost felt like his own damn heart was being ripped right out.

Going against his earlier notion to refrain from

touching her, he rested his hand against the small of her back. His hand practically splayed across the entire expanse, and something stirred inside him at the rightness of having Brianna there with him. Of feeling her delicate blouse beneath his rough fingertips. It was the only thing separating her soft skin from his touch. He shook his head, telling himself he was crazy. This would never end the way he wanted it to—with Brianna writhing beneath him, crying out his name—so why even pretend she was his to take care of?

Tonight he would, he decided. He wouldn't take her to bed, obviously, but he'd try to take her mind off the situation. Maybe talk about that marketing job she loved so much, or her fancy pants MBA. Brianna had always been whip smart, and even as a kid, he'd known she'd make something of herself. Not that he was doing so bad himself as a SEAL, but hell. He'd never be climbing up the corporate ladder like she was. Trudging through the desert and battling insurgents was more his line of work. Jumping out of airplanes? Yes. Giving PowerPoint presentations in a boardroom to a bunch of suits? Not a fucking chance.

"Let me buy you a drink," he said, guiding her toward the crowded bar.

He could see why she liked the place—it was more of a covered deck with views of the ocean than enclosed building. Waves crashed in the distance, "Margaritaville" cranked over the speakers, and the salty air soothed his soul. Laughter filled the space around them as they weaved their way through the crowd, the sounds of ice clinking in glasses mixing in with snippets of conversation.

Someday—one day far, far off in the future—he

wanted to own a place down by the water. Maybe here, maybe back in Virginia Beach. Just anywhere he could feel the sand beneath his feet and the ocean breeze on his face. And hell if he couldn't see a woman like Brianna right there with him. Imagine that.

"I'll have a rum and coke," Brianna said to the bartender. Matthew ordered a beer and guided her toward a vacant stool.

"There's only one seat," she protested.

"I'm fine," he assured her. Hell, after beating feet all over the damn planet, he sure the hell could stand here at the bar next to a pretty lady for an hour or two.

A college-aged girl in a skimpy dress and sky-high heels bumped into him as she walked by, and she turned to apologize. "It's fine, darlin'," he said. Brianna stiffened from her perch on the stool, and Matthew raised his eyebrows. Was she upset he was flirting with another woman?

The bartender brought over their drinks, and Brianna took a tentative sip of her rum and coke. Hell, she'd need a few more of those if he wanted her to relax and forget about things for the evening. He took a swig of his beer and leaned over to talk to her above the blare of the music. Her floral scent accosted him, invading his senses and making his mouth water with desire, but it was too late to pull away now. Her green eyes met his, and suddenly he felt lost in her again. Helpless to some imaginary pull she seemed to have. Would always have.

"Think your parents were upset that we left?" he asked, his voice gruff. He straightened up slightly, watching as her blonde hair rustled slightly in the breeze coming off the water.

"They were glad your folks came over. It's been a lot dealing with Beckett's injuries, flying back and forth between here and Walter Reed. I think they were happy for the company."

"It's been hard on everyone. Your folks especially. Mom couldn't wait to hustle us over there tonight though," he added with a chuckle.

"Yeah. I got the impression they were trying to push you and me together."

Matthew leaned against the bar and raised his eyebrows, his heart beating faster. Brianna looked flushed sitting on the barstool beside him, but he wasn't sure if it was from the alcohol, the crowd around them, or the idea of the two of them together. Which was absurd, anyway, because she was Beckett's sister. Besides, he was leaving again in two days, and who knew when the hell he'd return. He wasn't about to start something up that he could never see through.

He raised his beer to her. "To our mothers, darlin'," he said with a wink.

She turned an even deeper shade of pink but toasted him. Interesting.

"So tell me about this marketing position you have. Last time I talked to Beckett, it sounded like you were pretty hot stuff."

Brianna laughed nervously and shifted on the barstool, crossing those long legs. The dark denim hugged her curves, and his mouth watered at the thought of her legs wrapped around him as he drove into her.

*Making her come.*

What the hell was wrong with him? This was

Brianna. He'd never so much as kiss her, let alone have her in his bed. Beneath him. Begging.

He shifted as his cock hardened.

"Oh, Beckett was just bragging. Most of the other MBA candidates in my graduating class have entry-level marketing positions. I was managing this account, but...."

"But what?" he prodded.

"I don't want to bore you with the details," she said, flitting her hands nervously. "Tell me about you. You're up in Virginia now or something?"

"Little Creek," he agreed. "The Naval base near Virginia Beach."

"And, uh, will you be stationed there long?"

"Hopefully so. My team is the best—one of the best," he added, thinking of Beckett. "A few of my buddies are even coming in for Beckett's homecoming."

"Wow, seriously?"

"We're SEALs. He's a SEAL, and he's like a brother to me. Those guys have my back, on and off the battlefield. It's an honor for them to be there to show support at his homecoming. Lots of guys in his condition, well...."

"They don't survive," Brianna said quietly.

Matthew shook his head.

An upbeat song came blasting over the speakers, and Matthew decided he'd had enough of the somber mood. Plucking Brianna's drink from her hand, he ignored the surprised expression on her face and helped her down from the barstool, his large hand closing around her slender waist. Wordlessly, he led her over to the dance floor, loving a little too much the way her small hand fit in his. Like it freaking belonged there or something.

Other couples were happily laughing and swaying to the music, and it was about damn time the two of them let loose and had a little fun. They'd gotten away from their parents tonight for a breather, not to dwell on things they could never change. Dancing with Brianna, watching her tempting body sway to the music, would be dangerous, but Matthew wasn't so sure he could entirely stay away from her.

# Chapter 5

Brianna laughed as she and Matthew danced to the beat thumping over the speakers. He was surprisingly good on his feet for such a large guy, and she noticed more than a few women stealing glances his way. His large frame towered over hers, and even on the crowded dance floor, no one bumped into her with Matthew right there. His shirt stretched across his broad chest and shoulders, and the jeans he wore showcased muscular thighs. But it was the shimmy of his hips that drew her attention.

Damn.

This man would be amazing in bed—no doubt.

There was a small amount of dark stubble covering his jaw, and she unwittingly imagined what the feel of his whiskers rasping across her skin would be like. If she was smart, she would turn around and high tail it back over to the bar, grabbing a second drink. She'd do anything else but dance with the one

THE SEAL NEXT DOOR

man she'd dreamed about for most of her life.

A smile spread across his full lips as he watched her dancing, and his green eyes sparkled. This was the Matthew she remembered—fun, carefree, easygoing. Always up for a good time. Most of the time they'd spent together growing up had also involved Beckett. It was rare that she was ever alone with Matthew. But tonight? This was almost like her dream come true.

"You're a good dancer," Matthew shouted above the music.

"You too. Where'd you learn to dance like that?"

Matthew laughed. "You have to learn to dance when you're chasing after girls. While the other guys would sit around looking uncomfortable, I'd be the first one out on the dance floor."

Brianna shook her head. Yeah, that sounded like Matthew. Even as a teenager he had a trail of girls chasing after him. Had he ever had to pursue anyone? Unlikely. Matthew was a man used to calling the shots—having his way. If he wanted something, it was his. He'd seemed annoyed that she wouldn't let him drive her baby earlier. But seriously. She was a grown woman, perfectly capable of driving them around for the evening. And there was no way she was letting him boss her around. They sure the hell weren't kids anymore.

She raised her hands up above her head, dancing in time with the beat and swaying her hips back and forth. She felt Matthew's gaze slide over her as she moved almost as if it were a caress. Her breasts bounced up and down in the lightweight blouse she had on, and her shirt rose slightly up with her movements, revealing a sliver of her flat stomach. Hell, she worked hard to stay slim. Why not let loose a little tonight? And with the way she'd wanted Matthew practically forever, without him giving her so much as a second glance, she felt a certain satisfaction at having him finally look at her that way.

The music pulsed louder, and she shimmied around, feeling freer than she had all year. A breeze blew in from the ocean, and she lost herself in the music. Her job didn't matter. Dealing with the events of Sunday didn't matter. In this one moment, she didn't have a care in the whole world. The song finally came to a conclusion, and she grinned up at Matthew, who'd seemed to be having as much fun as her. A light sheen of sweat coated his skin, and he was real and raw and right in front of her.

Which was as close as he'd ever be.

A slower number came on, and before she could say a word, Matthew pulled her to him, his large hands spanning her hips. Thick fingers trailed over her jeans—sexy, powerful, and fully in control. Heat shot through her body at the way he handled her— like she was his to pull close. To dance with.

She glanced up at him, breathless, and was shocked to see the heat burning in his eyes. This was a mistake, such a mistake, but before she could pull away, he tugged her even closer and tucked her against his broad chest. She stiffened as she inhaled his clean, musky scent and felt his hard body pressed up against hers. Muscular arms wrapped around her, and he ducked down so his lips brushed against her ear.

"Relax, Brianna. It's just a dance."

"Matthew…."

"Just one dance," he said, his voice gruff as her body melded to his.

He held her gently as they swayed in time to the music, and she heard his pounding heartbeat beneath her ear. Matthew holding her felt like coming home—like she was safe and secure and nothing bad could ever happen.

That was just a fairytale though.

Her brother was injured, she'd lost her job, and she'd moved out of her apartment. Bad things happened every day, and one slow dance with the man she'd dreamed about since she was young wouldn't change that. One night with him wouldn't suddenly fix things.

His large hand slid to the back of her head, his fingers twining in her hair, and as she gazed up into his green eyes, she was lost. His grip around her waist tightened, and he managed to pull her even closer still. Matthew's arousal pressed against her belly, teasing her with every movement, and she felt a sudden dampness in her panties. Damn she wanted him. Needed him, even. His head moved a fraction of an inch closer, his eyes locked on her lips. The rest of the crowd on the dance floor seemed to evaporate.

"Brianna," he murmured, his voice husky and low.

Abruptly, she pulled back, feeling dazed. His eyes were surprisingly gentle as he watched her. What was happening here? She shouldn't be dancing like that with Matthew—like they were together or something. He shouldn't be holding her that way.

She took a shaky breath. "Let's get another drink," she suggested.

"Sure thing," he agreed. His hand lightly trailed down her arm as she turned away, almost as if he didn't want to let her go, and goose bumps covered her skin. He was barely touching her, but her entire body was buzzing with adrenaline and awareness. For him. If she wasn't careful, she'd let him consume her. And she wasn't a fool—Matthew was a SEAL just like her brother. He shipped out all over the world— or flew off on those damn loud planes that were always coming and going on base. And just like Beckett, he'd never had a serious relationship that she knew of. She could fall for him all over again, easily, but when he took off again, she'd be the one pining away for something that could never be.

Matthew's fingertips grazed her wrist, but she kept walking toward the bar, knowing he would follow. She tugged her hand away, breaking their connection, as she pushed her way back through the crowd. It took all her effort not to turn back.

***

Half an hour later she was laughing hysterically as Matthew finished telling her a sanitized version of his latest deployment as they relaxed back at the bar. Bugs crawling all over his tent, brutally hot weather, and day after day of disgusting MREs did not sound appealing to her. At all. But Matthew seemed to find humor in the situation—at least as he recounted his version of events to her. As a SEAL, she knew he couldn't tell her exactly where he'd been or what he'd been doing. Heck, she never knew where Beckett was most of the time. She didn't even know where he'd sustained the injuries that nearly cost him his life.

But here, tonight? None of that seemed to matter.

She finished her third rum and coke and watched Matthew's green eyes light up as he continued the story. Man, if he wasn't so freaking gorgeous, she could almost pretend she was just out with a friend for the night. That their slow dance earlier had never happened. She was comfortable with him in the way it always was when you'd known someone forever— now if only her heart didn't pound every time he leaned slightly closer to talk over the music.

Matthew's phone buzzed on the bar, and he glanced at the text message that popped up on the screen. "Just my buddies' flight info for tomorrow. Evan's already here, like I mentioned, but Brent is flying in then. Maybe Patrick. They're both on my SEAL team."

"I still can't believe they're coming down just for Beckett's arrival. Some of his SEAL team will be there, too, but that's different. Most of your friends don't even know him. Please make sure to tell your friends how much we appreciate it."

"Will do, ma'am," Matthew joked, a gleam in his eye.

"Ma'am?" she asked in mock astonishment.

Matthew smiled with a slow, sexy grin that spread across his face. Geez. No wonder women were always falling head over heels for the man. "Would you prefer darlin'?"

She laughed, trying to play it off. She wouldn't mind him whispering a whole bunch of sweet nothings in her ear. Not that she'd ever cop to that.

"Hell, I can't ever remember spending an entire evening alone with you," Matthew admitted. "It seems like Beckett was always around." He took a swig of his beer, appraising her.

"We did catch fireflies together one summer," Brianna mused with a smile. "Remember when Beckett broke his arm jumping out of that tree?"

Matthew howled with laughter. "Oh yeah. Think I dared him to do it, and he was mad as hell because he couldn't swim for the rest of the summer with his cast."

"He wasn't too happy with you then."

"We fought like brothers sometimes, but he's the best friend I've ever had."

The air between them shifted, and she knew they were both thinking about the what-ifs. What if Beckett had never come home? What if he wasn't the wall standing in their way? She stirred the tiny straw around in her drink.

"So what do you think Beckett will do once he recovers?" she finally asked.

"Well, active duty as a SEAL is out, for obvious reasons." Brianna saw a brief flash of concern cross his face, but it was gone just as quickly, and she almost wondered if she imagined it. "He could get a desk job if he wanted to stay in the military. There're plenty of defense contractors up in the DC area, but I imagine there's got to be some around base here, too. A guy as dedicated as him will find something. And hell, if that doesn't work out, maybe you could hook him up with a marketing job."

Brianna coughed, trying to mask her discomfort. Yeah, she'd need to find herself one of those first, she thought wryly.

"Another round?" the bartender asked as he approached them.

"Sure, I could go for another beer," Matthew said, his voice deep. "Bri?"

She did a double take at his calling her by her nickname. Some of her friends called her Bri, but to her family, it had always been Brianna. She kind of liked the way it sounded in Matthew's deep voice. It was almost…intimate. Like he had the right to call her something the rest of her family never did. "Sure, why not. I'll have a beer, too."

"Sure thing, darlin'." Matthew grinned at her, and she flushed. Was he flirting with her? Or was it just the alcohol talking? She had a feeling he wouldn't be teasing her like this if Beckett was around. He certainly wouldn't have pulled her close for a slow dance, tucking her against his chest like they were a couple or something. If he was smart, he would've dragged her back to the bar when a slow number came on, not pulled her tighter in his arms.

But if he was going to shamelessly tease her tonight, then two could play at that game. After all, all's fair in love and war.

"So did you leave a girlfriend behind at Little Creek?" she asked with an innocent smile.

Matthew looked taken aback for a moment and then shook his head slowly. "I'm not really the relationship type."

"You never have been," she agreed.

Matthew laughed, a loud chuckle that warmed her insides. "Been keeping tabs, huh?"

"What? No, nothing like that," she protested.

"I don't mind. If I was the type of man to settle down, it would be with someone like you."

She paused, her heart suddenly racing. Had he just admitted what she thought he did? "So you seriously don't think you'll ever get married?" She nervously played with her near-empty glass, listening to the ice clink.

Why did his answer suddenly matter so much? Like the whole world hinged on his response.

Matthew shook his head. "We deploy all the time. It works for some of the guys, maybe. But I couldn't leave a woman like that. I'd worry about her, and I need my head in the game. Guys make mistakes when their concentration is on something other than the mission. On the other men on their team. Plus, if I ever had kids….No, I just couldn't stomach being gone with my family at home wondering what happened to me, where I was, and when I'd be back. I wouldn't put a woman through that."

Brianna nodded, swallowing. Her skin tingled, and her stomach did a strange little flip. He almost looked regretful that he couldn't be in a relationship…almost like he wished he could start something with her.

Matthew watched her carefully, and she took a sip of the beer the bartender placed in front of her. This was crazy—the entire night had been surreal. Dancing with Matthew earlier, having a little heart-to-heart now. Tomorrow she'd wake up, and this entire conversation wouldn't even matter. It would be like it had never happened. So why, at the moment, did it feel like her heart was being crushed by something beyond her control? Matthew had left Pensacola years ago. Why pretend they could be something now?

Matthew licked his lips, looking more than anything like he wanted to bend down and kiss her. She knew he wouldn't—couldn't. But for the brief second their eyes met, an understanding passed between them. He could never give her what she wanted. The crazy thing was, he almost looked like he wanted it himself.

\*\*\*

Matthew walked Brianna back to the car an hour later, her keys dangling from his hand as he loosely draped his arm around her slender shoulders. She felt small and fragile beneath the bulk of his arm, and he felt a strange urge to pull her closer. To tuck her body against his and not let go.

The salty ocean breeze blew across the parking lot, and that combined with Brianna's light floral scent and that long blonde hair of hers tickling his skin as it blew in the wind?

Torture.

It stirred up all sorts of feelings he didn't want to acknowledge. Made him think of all sorts of futures he shouldn't contemplate.

Dancing with her had been heaven. The perfect excuse to pull her into his arms, if only for the evening. He'd never had an excuse to pull her close before. She'd been young and fresh-faced when he left to join the military. Cute in that sweet girl-next-door way, but not someone he could ever have. And to finally get a reason tonight to have her in his arms? Feeling those soft curves of Brianna's pushed up against him had been hell. Because she was everything he could never have.

Something had shifted between them after his revelation that he couldn't ever be in a relationship—he'd seen the interest and then inevitable disappointment in her eyes. It was crazy that out of all the women he'd ever been with, if he could settle down, Brianna might be the one. Life was just full of crazy shit, wasn't it?

"I had fun tonight," Brianna murmured sleepily, glancing up at him with those sea green eyes. "I didn't know you could dance like that. Wait until I tell

Beckett."

Matthew stiffened, recalling the slow dance where he'd held her closer than any man had a right to, and finally realized she was talking about before then, when they'd both let loose on the dance floor to the thumping music.

"Who do you think taught him his moves, darlin'?"

Brianna laughed, but Matthew cringed as he realized his error. Dancing. Wheelchair.

"Sorry, I didn't mean—"

"I know what you meant," Brianna assured him. "You guys always had a trail of girls chasing after you. It's no wonder."

Matthew glanced down at her in surprise, but she was already reaching for the door handle. He eased open the car door for her, helping her to settle inside. She let out a soft sigh as she nestled into the seat, and Matthew resisted the urge to bend over and buckle her seatbelt, brushing a kiss across her forehead.

Hell, he'd always watched out for her when they were kids. Kept an eye on her from afar as they grew older. But this? Damn. He wasn't cut out for what he was feeling now. Wanting to care for her, protect her. Make her his. He'd been home a few hours, and it felt damn near like his whole life had been turned upside down.

What would it be like cruising around Virginia Beach with Brianna in his pickup truck? Having her be a constant part of his life? They'd grab dinner, laugh over a few drinks. Then at night they'd pull up to the dunes tucked away on the beach, watch the sunset, and make love on a blanket under the stars.

Hell. Since when had he become so sappy?

He wasn't the type of man to "make love" to a woman. He enjoyed sex and giving the women he bedded pleasure, but it was for his satisfaction and theirs. Not some happily-ever-after type shit.

And even if he was the relationship type, he had no doubt Beckett would kick his ass for chasing after his younger sister. Missing leg be damned. He smirked at the thought. That was the first time he'd thought of his friend as "whole" again. Not felt sorry for him, not felt guilty over what he still had that Beckett didn't, but just imagined his buddy for what he was—a man. A brother. A Navy SEAL. And fucking hell if that didn't feel pretty damn spectacular. Maybe he could face everyone on Sunday without guilt eating him up inside after all. Maybe he could be there for Beckett—and Brianna.

"Thanks for driving," Brianna said sleepily as he slipped into the driver's seat.

"Anytime, sweetheart."

*Sweetheart.*

Where the hell had that come from? Somehow over the course of the evening he had started seeing her as something more. Something that never could be. He knew he'd run into her during his weekend home, but he'd half expected the little girl in pigtails—not the woman who looked so delightfully soft nestled into the car beside him. Not a woman he wanted to kiss and fuck and tease with pleasure all night long.

He shook his head, trying to get a grip. After adjusting the mirrors, he backed out of the parking space and turned on the radio, trying to drown out the muddled thoughts swirling in his head. Thank God Brent was flying in tomorrow. He'd go out with him and Evan for a drink or five. Watch Brent flirt with all the women and remind himself why starting anything up with Brianna would be pointless. A night out with his buddies was all he needed to get his damn head on straight. To remember his work. His mission. His duty as a SEAL.

Matthew muttered a curse under his breath as Brianna drifted off to sleep in the passenger seat.

He hadn't even been back in Pensacola one full day, and suddenly everything he'd been missing in his life was right here beside him. Trouble was, he couldn't have any of it.

# Chapter 6

Brianna yawned as she stood in line at the coffee shop down by the beach the following morning. The aroma of roasted beans filled the air, the Saturday morning crowd trickled in, and she wished it was a weekend in her former life—when she'd have the day off and not be getting ready to serve drinks all afternoon and evening.

She moved forward in line, her hair tickling her bare shoulder as her loose sweatshirt slipped to the side. Her mom had laughed earlier, telling her she looked like she'd stepped out of the eighties, Brianna remembered with a smirk. It was early on a weekend morning though—a loose sweatshirt and cropped yoga pants were par for the course.

Ordering a cappuccino and croissant, she stepped aside to wait for her coffee after she paid. It was amazing how after one unforgettable evening out with Matthew she could already be back to reality—

running her weekend errands, getting ready for another God-awful shift at the bar.

Memories of dancing with Matthew filled her mind, of his broad body moving in front of her. Of the way it had felt when he'd pulled her close. What had that been about anyway? Friends didn't slow-dance together—especially not when one of them was holding the other so tightly, it was almost as if he never wanted to let her go. She'd blame the alcohol, but Matthew had only had a beer at that point.

She'd actually fallen asleep on the short drive home, and when Matthew had gently rustled her awake, she could've sworn he'd called her sweetheart. Which really was crazy, because friends absolutely didn't call one another that. She'd had a few drinks, yes, but not enough to imagine the words coming from his mouth. Not enough to ignore the shift in the way he'd acted around her. Even after they'd pulled into her driveway, he'd walked her to the front door like they were on a date or something. The old Matthew never would've done something like that. They'd each wave goodbye and go their separate ways. This had almost felt like it meant something.

Not that it did. Or could.

After her cappuccino was ready, she wandered out to the boardwalk to eat her breakfast and watch the waves crash on the shore. She'd always found it peaceful down by the water—uplifting even. One day she'd dreamed of a fancy marketing career in a high-rise down by the ocean. She'd kill for a corner office with a view, although at the moment, just about any damn job in her field would be nice. She'd told her parents that she'd be out apartment hunting later this afternoon, but how many weekends of her doing that would they believe? Apartments weren't that hard to find. Night shifts at the bar were almost better because then at least she could claim she was out with friends or stuck at the office.

She took a sip of her drink, the warm, foamy confection seeping down her throat. A boat sailed by in the distance, and she felt a strange longing for that sort of freedom again—to pick up one weekend morning and do whatever she wanted. To spend the day however she chose. To have the money to actually afford such a luxury. As it was now, she was barely scraping by. And that was one thought she definitely did *not* want to linger on. Her old life had been comfortable. Cushy, even. She'd worked hard, but now something simple like grabbing gourmet coffee for breakfast felt like a splurge.

She sighed, watching some seagulls race over the water.

A shadow fell over her, looming large across the boardwalk, and she glanced back in surprise. The tall, hulking figure behind her caused her heart to race, but not in fear. Her breath caught, and she immediately felt her insides go molten.

Matthew's dark aviators hid his eyes, but his wide grin spread across his face. Well hell. Now she wished she'd dressed a little nicer for her morning coffee run. His dark hair still looked damp from the shower, and he'd shaved, showing off his strong jaw and chiseled features. Brianna took in his loose athletic shorts, running shoes, and zip-up sweatshirt. He looked like he was either ready for a morning of errands like her or ready for a run. Since he was only in town for the weekend, it was probably the latter.

"Care for some company?" he asked, holding up

his own cup of coffee.

"Sure, sit down," she said, hastily sliding over to make room for him. She felt oddly uneasy seeing him so early in the morning, when she was still half asleep. She was planning to mull over her future over coffee and a croissant, not be tempted by the irresistible man she'd known for a lifetime.

Matthew's body folded onto the bench beside her, and she caught a whiff of his aftershave. It was clean, slightly musky, and oh-too-delicious for her to be sitting this close to him. She needed her guard up so she could act like everything was fine. That he was the same as always—just the boy next door.

"Looks like we had the same idea," Matthew said, taking a sip of his drink. "Coffee, the beach, Saturday morning."

"Yeah, this is by far my favorite thing to do on a weekend morning. Almost makes getting out of bed worth it."

"Almost?" Matthew laughed.

"I wasn't planning on such a late night."

"I had fun," Matthew said huskily. She turned to face him but couldn't see his eyes beyond the dark glasses. How she'd kill to know what he was thinking.

A beat passed with neither of them saying a word. Finally, Matthew cleared his throat.

"I needed to fuel up with some caffeine before my run. I figured I'd grab some coffee, enjoy the view for a little while, and then get in a workout. I've got to pick up my buddy from base later on."

"How many guys are flying in?"

"Just Brent. Patrick—our SEAL team leader—was hoping to come down, but his son is sick, so he's not going to make it."

"Wow. I can't imagine doing what you guys do and having kids."

"Me either," Matthew said wryly.

Brianna took a sip of her cappuccino, trying not to stare at his muscular legs. Damn. Was any part of this man not perfection?

"How far do you usually run?" she finally asked.

"Ten miles on the weekend. Why, care to join me?"

"No way," Brianna said with a laugh. "I'm more of a gym girl anyway. I'm just grabbing breakfast before running some errands, then I have to get to work—uh, working on finding an apartment I mean."

Matthew nodded. "I'd tell you to look for a ground level unit, to make it easier for Beckett to visit, but they're not safe for a single woman."

"Oh, right," Brianna said in surprise. Geez. When she did ever move out, she'd have to take that into consideration. Her brother wouldn't be able to jog up a few flights of stairs to see her. Not now, and probably not ever.

"So I assume you'll have to get a building with an elevator then. Those are more expensive, but I'm sure it's not an issue with a great job like yours."

"Right," she agreed, watching an elderly couple stroll by holding hands. An odd sort of regret filled her chest, and she realized she felt guilty for lying to Matthew. He'd probably flip out if he knew she was serving drinks in a skimpy outfit night after night. She sure the hell knew her own brother had—and she'd convinced him that she'd left that job. It would be harder going along with the charade once he was home, living in the same house as her. But it wouldn't be for much longer, she reasoned. She'd find a great job soon enough and put her degree back to good use.

Matthew slipped his aviators atop his head and looked over at her. "Sorry, I wasn't trying to be bossy," he said with an easy grin.

"You? Never," she chastised.

"Guilty as charged I suppose. I just feel protective toward you. I mean, uh, you're Beckett's little sister and all."

Her smile faltered.

"Not that you're a kid anymore," he hastily continued. "I mean you're a grown woman. Uh…." He cleared his throat.

Brianna patted his thigh, feeling the corded muscle beneath his shorts. Holy hell. She quickly removed her hand. "Don't worry about it. I should get going anyway." She stood, Matthew quickly rising beside her. He towered above her, and she had to look up to meet his gaze.

"Bri, I didn't mean it like that. And I had fun last night, but—"

"I get it. I'll see you later," she said, turning away as she felt the pinpricks of tears in the corners of her eyes. Matthew hesitated, seeming unsure what to do, but he didn't follow as she walked away. It was for the best. Last night had been surreal—dancing with Matthew, letting him hold her in his arms. Rehashing the details of their relationship—one in which they were strictly friends and nothing more—wouldn't make her feel any better. Matthew had his own life back in Virginia. One which she had absolutely no place in.

\*\*\*

Brianna changed into her cocktail waitress dress back at the bar later that afternoon, ready for her long Saturday shift. She shoved her casual clothing into her locker and adjusted the zipper on her dress, fussing with the revealing outfit.

The black satin and lace frock dipped lower than she liked, showing off her cleavage to its fullest advantage, and the frilly skirt barely covered her bottom. Once she stepped into her heels, she'd be strutting around with her tits and ass waving around for all the customers to admire.

Just the way management liked it.

She blew out a sigh. Thank God she'd convinced her parents she'd be out apartment hunting all afternoon. If they knew she'd been laid off and was serving drinks while scantily clad in what looked more like lingerie than an actual uniform, they'd flip out.

She had a full eight-hour shift today, but the evening crowd always tipped the best. Hopefully in another month or so, she'd have nailed a new marketing position so that she could dust her hands of this waitressing business. She'd sent out ten resumes last week to potential leads but hadn't heard back yet from a single one. At least she was able to make her student loan and car payments with her current soul-sucking job. MBAs didn't exactly come cheap.

"Frank is managing tonight," Ella said as she slammed her locker shut next to Brianna. Her long, dark hair hung loose down her back, and without any makeup on, Ella looked even younger than usual in a tank top and leggings. Her willowy frame leaned against the wall as she sighed.

"Great," Brianna muttered. Ten years her senior, Frank had asked her out. Twice. The way his beady eyes slid over her body creeped her out, and she made sure she was never alone with him. Once after an all-hands meeting he'd invited her back into his office, but she'd made her excuses and fled. She shuddered to think of what he really wanted. He'd somehow managed to cage her in at the bar one night when she was getting drinks, and she'd nearly dropped the entire tray when she'd felt his hot breath on her neck. Creep.

"How'd the paper go?" Brianna asked as she touched up her lipstick. She fluffed her hair in the mirror, and the blonde waves she'd curled earlier framed her face. Her size D cups looked closer to DDs with the way the dress pushed up her breasts. God. She wasn't normally one to flaunt her assets, but she had to admit that the dress made her look good. Too bad it was more appropriate as something worn in the bedroom, in front of a lover, not in a roomful of males who had been drinking.

"Finished. Stayed up until 3:00 a.m., but it's done."

"When's it due?" Brianna asked in surprise.

"Monday morning. But I'm working a double shift tomorrow, and I needed it finished."

"Have you looked into scholarships or anything?" Brianna asked. Ella was working way too hard to put herself through school, she thought. She was going to burn the candle at both ends at this rate—working all weekend, taking extra classes each semester. At least once Brianna found another marketing job—hopefully sooner rather than later—she could move on with her life. Ella might be stuck working here for years while she finished her degree. It paid better than many other hourly jobs, but she knew Ella hated it as much as she did.

"Not yet. Maybe this summer I'll check them out again when I have some extra time."

"What about a job on campus?"

"The pay sucks there," Ella said, slipping on her identical dress. "This job is crap, but it pays my tuition."

Brianna blew out a sigh. Yeah, it paid tuition and student loans, but there was only so much she could take.

They finished getting ready and walked out into the hallway to start their shifts, almost bumping right into their manager. Frank's eyes slid down Brianna's body, lingering appreciatively on Brianna's chest, and she fought the urge to slap him in the face. That was a sure way to get herself fired. But then again, wasn't it some form of sexual harassment to have her boss leer at her that way?

He smelled of stale cigarette smoke and booze, his normally crisp khakis and button-down shirt looking rumpled. Even though smoking wasn't allowed in the club, the back patio had plenty of tables for customers. Although Frank had been known to sneak out for a few minutes for a cigarette break from time to time, the scent of alcohol coming off of him was unusual. Not to mention unsettling. He looked like he wanted to say something to Brianna, but his gaze slid briefly over to Ella, and he simply nodded at both women before brushing past them on the way into his office.

"That was awkward," Ella muttered.

"No kidding," Brianna agreed, walking out into the already crowded bar. "He creeps me out."

"I don't like the way he looks at you," Ella proclaimed.

Brianna raised her eyebrows. "Me either. I sent out a ridiculous number of resumes last week; hopefully I'll be out of here sooner rather than later."

"I hope you find something, but God, I'll miss you when you go."

Brianna scanned the room, grateful that she had tomorrow off. The bar was nearly filled, mostly with men, and the customers were watching sports on TV, enjoying their beverages, and chowing down on appetizers. Hearty laughter filled the air, and Brianna had a feeling this would be a long night. She grabbed the notepad from her frilly apron and said goodbye to Ella, heading over to cover her first table. Her section wasn't too crowded yet, but she could see Ella was already swamped with a large group of rowdy college students. Perfect.

It was only four, and she was on the clock until eleven. Brianna dreaded Saturday nights here the most, when the crowds seemed to drink even more. The men would get handsy, the women belligerent, and it was all she could do not to dump their drink orders right over their heads. How anyone had the patience to be a waitress for any extended period of time was beyond her. The tips were good, but that was about the only redeeming quality. She had high hopes that she'd hear back from a couple of prospective employers next week and get the hell out of here.

A young guy smiled at her as she approached the table, his heated gaze sliding down over her breasts, and she resisted the urge to cringe. This job might not be so bad if they didn't have to wear such skimpy outfits. Half the men looked at her like they wanted to bend her over the nearest table and have their wicked way with her.

Her cheeks pinkened at the thought.

She could always waitress somewhere else, but then she'd have to sell her car and would barely be able to make her student loan payments. And she needed a car to get to a job, so…unless a new marketing career landed in her lap, this was it for the moment.

"What can I get for you, gentlemen?" she asked, plastering on a smile. *Right. As if a real gentleman would openly ogle her like that.*

"You in my bed for a start," another guy at the table said, chuckling.

"Uh-uh," the first guy protested, reaching over and grabbing her wrist before she could pull away. His calloused thumb slid across her skin, and she tried not to cringe. "I saw her first."

Brianna politely tugged her hand back and poised her pen above the notepad. "Drinks guys."

The men placed their orders, the first guy still openly leering at her cleavage, and she turned and walked across the room toward the bar. If this was the way her entire shift was going to go, it was going to be a long night. The bar served up drinks, not women, but a few men had been known to get the wrong idea from time-to-time, tugging a pretty waitress into his lap and asking for something more. Her annoying manager Frank was always quick to put a stop to that sort of thing, but that didn't make it any more comfortable when it happened.

Loud laughter from another section caught her attention, and her gaze landed on a group of men.

Navy, from the looks of it. The bar was near Naval Air Station Pensacola, and it wasn't unusual for a group of men in uniform to come in. They'd usually flirt with the female customers and pretty waitresses while they enjoyed a few drinks. Brianna knew a few ladies she worked with who'd go home with one of the sailors for the night. Not that Brianna did the one-night-stand type thing. Ever. But who was she to fault the others if that's what they were looking for?

Her gaze skimmed over a menacing-looking man with jet black hair, a younger guy who was blond, and finally landed on a muscular guy with brown hair. A man whose build she'd recognize anywhere. Her face flamed and heart raced as he took a swig from his bottle of beer.

*What on Earth was Matthew doing here?*

The dark haired guy at his table let out a whistle at a group of women walking by. Matthew ignored them, continuing to talk to his other friend, as the women approached other guy, laughing.

Shakily, Brianna forced herself to continue walking to the bar to hand over her drink orders.

"Are you okay, hun?" the female bartender asked, eyeing her curiously.

"Oh, uh, great," Brianna said, turning away.

She felt dizzy and ill at the idea of Matthew spotting her. Of him thinking less of her for prancing around in a skimpy outfit and serving cocktails to make a living. Thank God he wasn't in her section, but how was she going to avoid him the entire night? It was crowded, yes, but she had drinks to serve and customers to attend to. She couldn't be ducking every time she was worried that she'd be in his line of vision. And it wasn't like he'd sit there at the table with his buddies forever, ignoring the rest of the bar. They'd probably work the room, flirting with the women as the night wore on.

And if he spotted her in this outfit? Game over. Not only would she utterly die of embarrassment, but she'd never hear the end of it. From him or Beckett.

Ella approached the bar, pushing her hair out of her face. "I got stuck with a table of twelve college guys. Can we say lousy tippers?" She glanced over at Brianna. "Hey, are you feeling okay? You're white as a ghost."

"Oh, yeah, I'm fine," she said, swallowing the lump in her throat. "Just felt dizzy for a second there."

"Maybe you should go home. You look kind of pale," Ella said, eyeing her skeptically.

Brianna shook her head, plastering a smile on her face. "It's nothing I can't handle. I should get to my other tables." She quickly turned and walked off, leaving Ella standing there, looking bewildered. She purposefully looked away from Matthew's table as she made her way back across the room in case he glanced over. This was absurd. She couldn't hide from him all evening. She really was going to have to leave early—faking illness, pretending she was injured, anything. After this next table, she was out of here.

\*\*\*

Matthew laughed as he took a pull from his longneck. The cold, hoppy brew slid down his throat, and he found himself relaxing for the first time all day. The bar he and his buddies had popped into was crowded for late Saturday afternoon, but he could easily see why. Pretty waitresses in sexy little dresses made the rounds, serving up plenty of beers and strong cocktails. Giant flat-screen TVs had the games on, and the appetizers and burgers they served were pretty damn good. Men and women alike were trickling in through the front door, and he had a feeling that had he been looking, this was easily the type of place where he could pick up a woman to bring home for the night.

Instantly, his mind flashed back to Brianna.

Hell, she was exactly the woman he wanted to take home for a night. Maybe take home forever. But that was never going to happen in this lifetime. He'd enjoy a few beers with his buddies, see his best friend tomorrow, and then move the hell on with his life.

The trouble was, his little apartment back in Little Creek was seeming a lot lonelier now after spending an evening with Bri yesterday. After running into her down by the beach this morning. Hell, it had taken everything in him not to duck down and kiss her as they'd sat at the bar yesterday. Just to see how she tasted—to watch how she'd react. Beckett would no doubt kill him for moving in on Brianna, but he had a feeling it would be well worth the hell he'd have to pay.

Too bad chasing after her wasn't a damn option.

"Sorry, but I'm taken," Evan said to a group of giggling women who were currently flirting with Brent.

"Aw, but so you're so cute," one of them purred.

"I'll be sure to tell my girlfriend that," Evan joked.

Matthew had picked up Evan from his hotel and Brent from base an hour ago. Their CO had been good to allow the three of them to head down here for the weekend, but the military was a tight-knit group, especially amongst the men who called themselves Navy SEALs. Hell, it would be good to have some of his team there tomorrow to give his buddy a proper welcome home. Beckett certainly needed to see how many people were rooting for his recovery.

Their waitress came over and asked if they wanted another round. "Hell yeah," Brent said. "Keep 'em coming."

"Sure thing, sailor," she said with a wink. "Are you guys from base?"

"I'm only down here twenty-four hours, gorgeous. Know anywhere I can spend the night? I prefer not to sleep alone," he added with a wicked grin.

She cocked her head to the side, appraising him. "Something tells me you wouldn't have trouble finding a woman to spend the night with. What happened to the group of ladies that was just over here?"

"Bachelorette party," he explained. "But I don't want just any woman, princess. What time does your shift end?"

She laughed but bent over, thrusting her cleavage right into Brent's face as she whispered something in his ear. His smile grew a mile wide, and Matthew shook his head in disbelief.

"Be right back with your drinks, boys," she said with a sultry smile as she sashayed away.

Evan raised an eyebrow. "What the hell was that about?"

"Sorry, Flip, you're on your own back at the hotel tonight. I'm crashing over at Brittany's place. Hell, what cup size do you think those babies were? DD at least. They looked fucking spectacular."

"Good God," Matthew muttered. Brent was known for his insatiable appetite for women. Although Matthew hadn't exactly been opposed to it in the past, spending weekends with his buddies hitting on pretty ladies, lately the one-night-stands he'd enjoyed hadn't seemed as fulfilling. Sexually, maybe, but he couldn't wait to get out of there afterward. Spending the entire night taking pleasure in a woman was turning into a thing of the past, and he was earning a reputation as more of a wham-bam-thank-you-ma'am type. Which wasn't exactly his intention, but hell. He wasn't looking to marry the woman he went home with either.

"Looks like they'll have an empty room back at the hotel," Brent said, a gleam in his eye. "You find someone to take home tonight, Gator, and it's yours."

Matthew laughed as Brent called him by his nickname. "The ladies here are attractive; I won't fault you that. But I'm home for the weekend staying with my folks, not for a booty call."

"There are some damn fine booties here," Brent taunted, his eyes flicking around the crowded bar.

"Not tonight," Matthew said.

"Buzz kill," Brent muttered.

Evan's phone vibrated on the table, and he glanced down at the screen, concern etching across his face. "Shit. Ali's sick again."

Matthew raised his eyebrows. Although Evan had confided in him about the pregnancy, he wasn't sure if the rest of the team knew.

Brent caught the look that passed between them. "Everything okay, man?"

"Yeah. Ali's pregnant," Evan confessed.

Brent howled with laughter. "Pregnant? Shit! You, my man, are whipped. Pussy whipped."

"Don't be an ass," Evan muttered.

Matthew chuckled and looked over at Brent. "They live together, asshole. It was bound to happen sooner or later. Apparently some people want all that happily-ever-after shit."

"Hell, you and I are the only single men left on the team," Brent said in disbelief. "You sure as shit better not go deserting me, turning all soft over some woman."

Matthew took another swig of his beer and grinned. "No chance of that."

Brent guffawed. "What about the woman from last night?"

"My next-door neighbor?"

"The very one," Brent agreed. "It's not like you to crash and burn after a night out. Did she shoot you down or something?"

Matthew felt his gut clenching, wishing he'd never filled them in on his first night back in town. "Nah, nothing like that," he said, trying to keep his cool. "She Beckett's kid sister. A grown woman now, perhaps, but off-limits." He met Brent's gaze, ensuring that Brent knew she was off limits to him, too. That's all needed, Brent hitting on Brianna tomorrow. And he would, too, no matter who he spent the night with tonight. The woman was completely gorgeous.

"What's she look like anyway?" Brent asked, evidently having similar thoughts.

"None of your damn business," Matthew snapped.

Good God. Why was he getting himself so worked

up over what Brent said? Brianna could date whoever the hell she wanted. Because it would never be him.

Brent began chatting with a pretty redhead that walked over to their table, and Evan was texting Ali back. Matthew drained the rest of his beer and scanned the restaurant, his eyes falling on a pretty blonde waitress working her way between the tables. Her hair was almost the same as Brianna's, but it fell in pretty waves down past her shoulders. The way she moved in that sexy-as-fuck dress was a sight to behold, and he let his eyes wander over her gorgeous figure.

She turned and bent over to retrieve some plates from one table, and although her face was blocked from his view, his mouth watered at the tempting sight off all that ample cleavage put on display. Hell. He'd promised himself he'd be good for the weekend, but this woman was making him regret that. If he couldn't have Brianna, maybe he could spend a couple of hours taking his pleasure in another woman—and sending her soaring as well.

He was the type of man that prided himself in giving a woman pleasure. He loved hearing the woman he was with moan out his name as he made her come. Hell, to have Brianna's soft curves beneath him, to have his name on her lips, to have his cock buried so deep inside her tight—wait, what the hell was wrong with him? That chick wasn't Brianna, just some smoking hot waitress that worked here. And looked a bit like her. She probably had men hitting on her left and right with that gorgeous body.

He watched as she reached for an empty glass across the table, her breasts bouncing in the low-cut dress, and he felt an unfamiliar stirring inside his chest. Possessiveness. Protectiveness. Which was completely crazy considering he didn't even know the woman.

Brent finished chatting up the redhead and followed his gaze across the room, his mouth breaking into a wide grin. "You got your eyes on that pretty blonde? Because her tits are spectacular."

Matthew's gaze swept to the side. So what if Brent commented on the woman he'd noticed? That dude hit on every female in sight. But he didn't like that Brent's attention was now fully focused on his woman. *His woman.* Yeah right. He didn't know this chick, and she sure the hell wasn't his.

Matthew's fist clenched as she stood, and her blonde hair swung to the side. It was impossible, but from this angle, she looked exactly like Brianna. Same height, same hair, same gorgeous figure. She started to walk away with her full tray when a man from another table grabbed onto her waist. She turned in surprise, balancing her heavy load, and Matthew's chest tightened as his blood ran cold.

What the fuck was Brianna doing here?

# Chapter 7

Brianna almost stumbled in her high heels, balancing the heavy tray of plates and glasses, as some drunk idiot grabbed onto her waist, attempting to pull her over to his table. Jesus. It was only, what, six? He must've been downing beers for hours to already be in this state. Couldn't he wait patiently for her to get to his table like everyone else?

She plastered a smile on her face. "I'll be right with you. Let me go drop this off first."

"A round of shots for my buddies and me," he said, his gaze slightly unfocused.

"Sure thing."

"Tequila," he added.

"No problem. I'll be right back with your shots."

She tugged away, somehow maintaining her hold on the tray, and carried the dirty glasses and plates back to the kitchen. She dropped the tray onto the counter, listening to the loud clatter echoing in the already noisy kitchen. A few people glanced her way, and she rested her hands on the counter, blowing out a sigh. She'd asked Frank if she could leave early, feigning illness, but he'd all but implied her job was as good as over if she left tonight. She knew she was leaving him in a lurch by asking to duck out on the busiest night of the week, but she'd never left early before.

The stress of circumnavigating the room to avoid Matthew was grating on her nerves as well. Her arms had shook as she'd carried the heavy tray clear around his general area to avoid detection, which was ridiculous. She had customers to attend to, drinks to serve. She couldn't spend her whole night trying to avoid him—which was exactly why she'd wanted out of here. Pronto. Maybe she could get her parents to call, saying she was needed at home or something. Yeah right. And explain to them why she was working here?

She walked back out to the bar, exasperated, and requested a round of shots.

"Sure thing, hun," the female bartender said, sending her a sympathetic gaze. "Someone giving you problems?"

"No, just a long night. Afternoon. Whatever."

"Does it have anything to do with those guys over at table 20?"

"What? No," Brianna said, feeling herself flush as she thought of Matthew and his friends. Good God. Was it that obvious that she'd been watching them?

"One of them keeps glancing over here like he's seen a ghost."

"I'm sure it's nothing," she mumbled, feeling her heart rate speed up. Crap. Had Matthew seen her?

"I'll get those shots for you."

Brianna's gaze slid over the people talking and laughing too loudly, and it was all she could do not to turn around and leave despite her manager's warning. This job sucked. At the moment she wanted nothing more than to simply disappear.

The bartender nodded at her, indicating her shots were ready, and Brianna lined up the glasses on a round tray. Six shots for six assholes, she thought wryly.

She turned, weaving her way between all the tables, and suddenly felt a pair of eyes boring into her. A shiver raced down her spine, and she paused, scanning the restaurant. The men at the table who'd ordered the shots were distracted, talking to some women nearby. Her eyes discreetly swept to the side, a feeling of dread washing over her. She was supposed to be sticking to the edges of the restaurant, avoiding attention. And she knew, without even looking directly his way, that he'd spotted her. In her haste she'd taken the quickest route to her table—and walked right into his line of sight.

Her heart pounded as Matthew's green eyes drilled into hers. He looked angry enough to crush the tumbler of whiskey he was currently holding and about ten seconds away from marching across the room and hauling her out of there with him. Waves of embarrassment washed over her, and she shakily carried the tray of drinks over to her table, finally pulling her eyes from Matthew's steely gaze. She knew he was watching her every move, and that made her even more nervous.

Finally she reached her table and hastily handed placed the first shot down. The sooner she delivered their order, the sooner she was out of here. Consequences be damned.

"Is there a private room here, sweetheart?" the drunk guy who'd ordered the tequila shots asked.

"No, this is a cocktail lounge."

"I'd love some time alone with you," he slurred.

She nearly dropped the tray as his hand slid up her short skirt and he palmed her bottom, covered only in satin panties. She jumped a foot in the air, trying to ease away from him, but the room was crowded and she had nowhere to go. He tried to guide her closer to him and flustered, she turned away, pushing through the crowd, drinks spilling over on the tray. She caught the look of alarm on Matthew's face as she headed back in his direction toward the bar, but she ignored him, shoving her tray full of drinks across the bar and rushing into the private hallway that led to the offices and employees' locker room.

The hall was dimly lit, and the sounds from the restaurant faded into the background as her hands shook and she struggled to catch her breath. Tears pricked the corners of her eyes, and she willed herself not to cry. *God.*

First Matthew had seen that she *worked* here, that she'd been lying about her marketing job, and then some creep had just groped her. She cringed as she recalled the feel of his large hand covering her panties. As he'd tried to guide her even closer to him. She'd been in a room full of people yet felt trapped— too shocked to even scream. There just wasn't any way today could get any worse.

She heard the thumping of footsteps behind her and knew that Matthew had followed her down the secluded hall. She'd have to talk to him sooner or later, but now wasn't the time. All she wanted to do was get out of there and go home. Change out of this God-awful outfit and burn it or something. Matthew would just have to—

"Well, this looks promising," a deep voice slurred from behind, and she froze, her blood running cold.

That wasn't Matthew. Which meant that some asshole had followed her back here. Back where she was completely alone. Where even if she screamed, she wasn't sure if anyone would hear.

The thumping of music from the main bar area sounded dull in the hallway, and her stomach churned. Cameras were mounted discreetly on the walls, but with a big Saturday night crowd, Frank was likely out working the floor, not monitoring the feed from his office while he did paperwork.

And would he really come to her rescue anyone? With the creepy way he always looked at her, practically undressing her with his eyes, he'd probably enjoy the show.

Her mind raced through her limited options. She could run into the locker room, but what if he followed her? That was even more secluded unless someone walked in on them. She could try to shove past him back into the restaurant where all the people were. No, her best bet was to run out the emergency exit. It would sound the alarm, but at least she'd get away. The back patio wasn't far from there, and she could find someone to help her. Her head swung toward the door, the red "EXIT" sign hanging above.

She could do it. She could run.

Heavy footsteps pounded down the hallway, and she heard ringing in her ears as her pulse raced in a panic. She turned and started to run, but the drunk guy was behind her in an instant, his hands roughly gripping her upper arms as he pushed her against the wall. She cried out, her face and breasts pressing against the rough brick, and one large hand covered her mouth as she struggled against him. He gripped her arm tighter, to the point where she knew she'd have bruising tomorrow.

"Take it easy, sweetheart. You know you're asking for it in that skimpy little outfit you have on. You're lucky I didn't rip it off you right at the table."

He laughed too loudly and swayed slightly behind her from the alcohol he'd been drinking. She tried to move away but his body pressed closer, pinning her to the wall. She felt the hardness of his erection behind her, digging into her lower back, and choked out a sob. His hand sank into the ruffled skirt of her dress.

Tears streamed down her face as she tried to push back, to push him away, but he was too strong. His large body caged her in, and she felt his warm breath on her neck just as his clumsy fingers skimmed against her inner thigh.

"I've been wanting to have some fun with you all night long," he leered, pulling her head back against his shoulder, his hand still drowning out her whimpers. "Should we do it here or in the back of my truck? I want at least an hour with you."

"Get off her!" Matthew suddenly shouted, his voice echoing off the walls.

Brianna began struggling again, waves of relief washing over her. Matthew was here. He wouldn't let this asshole hurt her.

"Wait your turn," the drunk guy slurred. His hand rose higher up her inner thigh, edging closer to her panties, but he released his grip on her mouth just enough so that Brianna bit down on his hand. Hard.

He screamed as he jumped back and then he was crashing against the wall, thrown down by Matthew, who'd charged at them like a raging bull.

Her attacker crumpled to the ground as Matthew roughly grabbed the man's shirt, pulling him up and tossing him down again as he cursed. Blood came gushing from a gash in his forehead where skin had scraped against exposed brick. The other men from Matthew's table came rushing down the hall a second later, and the dark-haired one restrained the drunk man on the ground while the blond guy pulled out his cell phone and called the police.

"Brianna."

Matthew gently reached out to her, and shaking, Brianna collapsed against his broad chest. She didn't want him to see her like this, but at the moment, she needed him more than she needed her next breath. She inhaled his warm, musky scent as his shirt became damp with her tears. He shucked off the light jacket he was wearing, wrapping it around her.

Brianna trembled, and Matthew's muscular arms tightened as he held her in his firm embrace. "God damn it, Bri, I swear my life just flashed before my eyes when I saw that asshole touching you. Do you know what could've happened if I hadn't gotten here in time?" His voice cracked with emotion, and Brianna let her sobs escape.

All the pent-up frustration from the past few weeks, all the fear she'd experienced in the last few moments, escaped as she clung to Matthew like he was her lifeline.

"I know…I didn't—I couldn't.…"

"Shhh," Matthew soothed. "You're safe now."

His large hand moved up and cradled the back of her head as the other securely held her to him. Brianna felt dizzy and weak as the adrenaline that had been surging through her moments before all drained away. If it wasn't for Matthew holding her up, she didn't think she'd still be standing. And if he hadn't gotten here in time—she shuddered, not even wanting to think of the end result.

Humiliation and embarrassment washed over her now that she was safe. She could hear Matthew's friend—probably his SEAL team buddy—calmly relaying the information to the police dispatcher. What would his friends think of her now, she wondered? They'd flown down to Pensacola to support her brother, and she sure as hell hadn't intended to meet them like this—being attacked by a drunk guy as she'd been waitressing in the very cocktail lounge they decided to stop by.

"I'll fucking kill you!" the drunk guy shouted, and Brianna jumped in Matthew's arms.

"Don't give me a reason to break your neck," the SEAL holding him down growled. Matthew guided her away from the scene as the guy further dug his knee into the attacker's back, causing him to wince in anguish.

"The police are on the way," his other friend called out. "ETA is under five minutes."

"I'm taking you home," Matthew said quietly, his voice deep as his lips hovered by her ear. "I need to make sure you're safe—that he didn't hurt you. And then I want you to tell me exactly what the hell you're doing here."

# Chapter 8

Matthew's jaw tightened as he leaned against the exposed brick wall, waiting for Brianna to finish changing in the locker room. The scent of stale cigarette smoke hung in the air, drifting in the vents from the patio out back. A light flickered above him, and he resisted the urge to pound on the door, hauling Brianna out himself. Just so he could assure himself that she was unharmed.

Her dick of a manager had come by a few minutes ago, and it was all Matthew could do not to slug him in the face. What the hell kind of place was he running, having the women prance around in skimpy little outfits without any type of security? Maybe they were only serving drinks, but hell, they were asking for trouble mixing alcohol and scantily clad women. Some guys had no self control—no respect for women. A bouncer or two at the door could have prevented some of what had happened tonight. If

Matthew hadn't been there, who knows what the hell that asshole would have done to Brianna.

Scratch that.

Matthew knew, and he shuddered just thinking of it.

Just seeing that asshole slipping his fingers up Brianna's dress had made him see red, and the way that the tears had streamed down her face as he'd held her against her will had nearly slayed him.

He pounded one fist into his open palm impatiently, wondering what was taking Bri so long. He hadn't want to let her out of his sight, and the only reason he'd let her go into the locker room without him by her side was that she had a friend with her. That willowy college-aged girl that had followed Bri in there didn't look like she could harm a fly, but she also didn't look like she could protect Brianna from any danger. At least she wasn't in there alone. But what was the hold up? Was she…crying? Scared? Afraid to come out?

His chest clenched at the thought.

Damn. It was a good thing Beckett wasn't in town, because as much as Matthew had wanted to inflict more bodily harm on her attacker, there probably would've been no stopping Beckett. Missing leg or not.

Matthew glanced back down the hall, watching as the police finally led the attacker away in handcuffs. About damn time. At least that asshole wouldn't be here when Bri finally emerged.

Evan and Brent walked up to him, both looking madder than hell. "How's Brianna?" Evan asked, his brow creasing. "Is she still changing?"

Matthew blew out a sigh. "Yep. I'm still waiting

for her."

"It's too bad the police got here so quickly," Brent spat out. Matthew raised his eyebrows, waiting for the kicker.

"I would've taken that mother-fucker out with my bare hands," Brent continued.

Matthew grimly nodded, not doubting for a second Brent's anger. Brent's own sister had been killed by a jilted ex-boyfriend, and of all the men on his team, he didn't take that sort of thing lightly. Hell, none of them would stand for a man harming a woman. Ever. And the fact that it had been Brianna in danger? Well, that affected Matthew even more than he wanted to admit to himself.

"Who's the dude in the suit?" Matthew asked, nodding at a slick looking older gentleman that had arrived and was currently talking to a uniformed cop.

"The asshole's lawyer," Brent said. "He hasn't even been hauled off to prison yet, and his lawyer shows up."

"Figures," Matthew muttered. "He probably keeps him on retainer for all the trouble he causes."

"Aren't there cameras?" Evan asked, eyeing the discreet sensors mounted on the walls. "He shouldn't be able to get away with anything if the attack is on tape."

Matthew nodded, his gut churning. They very last thing he ever wanted to see was a replay of the night's events. It would haunt his nightmares as it was. He'd seen a lot of hell in his days in the military, but to see the woman he love—wait. What the hell was he thinking? He wasn't in love with Brianna. He cared about her, yes, and he'd die if anything had happened to her.

He swallowed, realization slowly dawning on him.

The discussion Evan and Brent were having on the security footage faded into the background as Brianna finally emerged from the employee locker room, eyes red, her large handbag clutched in her trembling hands. Matthew's heart clenched as he crossed the hall toward her. She looked younger than usual, her face scrubbed free of the heavy makeup she'd been wearing. Now in jeans and a lightweight tank top, her blonde hair floating around her shoulders, she looked young. Fragile. He wanted to pull her close and protect her. Keep her safe. Never let her go.

Her lower lip trembled as she met his gaze.

"Are you okay?" he asked quietly, ducking his head down to meet her eyes. Who cared if his buddies were watching? He didn't care if the whole damn world saw his concern for Brianna—as long as she was safe. That was all that mattered right now.

"Yeah. Can you drive me home?" She swiped a stray tear from her cheek, and he longed to thumb it away himself. To caress her soft skin.

"Of course."

Brianna's friend followed her out of the locker room a moment later. She'd also changed back into regular clothes and had pulled her long dark hair up into a ponytail. "Should I tell Frank we're outta here?"

"He knows," Matthew said, his voice steel.

Evan and Brent crossed the hallway to join them. "You need us for anything, Gator?" Brent asked. "Otherwise we're gonna split."

"You're leaving your lady friend?" Evan asked.

"Nah. I'll catch up with her later. She gave me her address."

"Christ," Matthew muttered. He glanced from Brianna over to his buddies. "I'm going to drive Brianna home. Think you guys can rustle up a cab or something?

Brent nodded, his eyes narrowing as he looked over at Brianna's friend.

Matthew followed Brent's gaze. "Are you okay getting home…?" he asked.

"Ella," she said, sticking out a slender hand.

"Matthew," he replied, grasping her hand in his. "This is Evan and Brent," he said, gesturing to the guys behind him.

She nodded, looking at the men somewhat warily. They did make an imposing group, but hell. She should know she had nothing to be afraid of. "Yeah, I'm fine. My car's out back, so I'll walk out with you guys if that's okay."

"I'm in the front, but we'll walk you out," Matthew assured her.

A door slammed down the hall, and Frank came stomping out of his office, looking furious. The two policemen that he'd been speaking with were already headed out the back emergency exit as Frank stormed in their direction. "Why the hell are you back here?" he asked Ella as he caught sight of her. "Why aren't you wearing your uniform?"

She jumped a foot in the air, and before Matthew could confront their angry manager, Brent stepped in, blocking Ella's small frame with his.

"Both of them are leaving right now," he growled.

"But I need her—"

"If you have a problem with it, you're going to have to deal with me first."

Frank did a double-take, backing away from

Brent's imposing figure. "Well, don't expect a paycheck, Ella," he snapped, storming off down the hall as he headed back to the restaurant.

"Jerk," she muttered.

Brent moved to follow him, but Evan gripped his forearm, muttering, "Not now."

"What the hell's wrong with him?" Brianna asked, her voice wavering. "He can't expect you to stay here after what happened tonight. And he has to pay you."

Ella shrugged. "Don't know, don't care. But you're not the only one quitting tonight."

Matthew nodded tightly. "Let's get going then. We'll walk you out."

He made a move to head toward the back door, but Brent stopped him. "I'll walk Ella to her car. Then Evan and I can catch a cab back to the hotel."

Matthew slid his gaze between Brent and Ella.

"Where are you guys staying?" Ella asked. She didn't look so frightened anymore, actually more relieved than anything. Maybe it was good they were there to stand up to her manager, to show her not all men were jerk-offs. That some guys actually respected women and would protect them, not harm them.

Evan swiped his phone and read the hotel's address. "That's right on my way," she said. "I'll drop you guys off. I'd feel better not being alone right now."

They agreed and all walked out the back together. The cooler air outside felt refreshing, and without the noise from the crowd, TVs, and music, it was pretty damn peaceful. Aside from the fact that they were still standing mere feet from where Brianna had been assaulted. The sooner Matthew got her out of here, the better he'd feel. After saying their goodbyes,

Matthew escorted Brianna around the side of the restaurant to his car. There was no way he was taking her back in there.

They rounded the side of the building to the front parking lot, walking over to his empty car. He unlocked the doors as Brianna scanned the lot. When she caught sight of the one remaining police cruiser, she immediately burst into tears.

"Hey," Matthew said, pulling her into his embrace. "It's okay. Everything's okay now." Her small frame trembled in his arms, and he ducked his head low, inhaling the floral scent of her blonde waves. He ran his fingers through her soft strands, wishing more than anything that he could comfort her. Kiss her. Take her tears away.

Brianna pulled back and swiped the teardrops streaming down her cheeks. "It's not okay. Nothing's okay. I lost my job, all right? The great marketing one that you keep asking me about? I got laid off, which is why I'm working in this shitty place. I had to move out of my apartment, Beckett's injured, and now with Frank claiming we won't even get paid, I won't be able to make my student loan payments this month."

"Is that why you're working here? Bri, I'll loan you the money. Hell, I'll even pay the bill for you. God knows I'm not spending all the money I earn from deploying all over the damn world. Hazard pay for a single guy adds up quickly."

"I don't want your money," Brianna said, crying harder. "I want my old job back—my old life. I shouldn't need anyone to help me."

Unable to stop himself, Matthew cupped her face in his hands, wiping away the tears that still fell. "Bri," he said softly. "I wish I would've known—I know I haven't seen you in years, but hell. I'd always help you. I hate that you were working here."

Brianna nodded, her tears beginning to slow. "So did Beckett."

Matthew did a double take. "Beckett knew you were working here? And he didn't try to stop you?"

"No, he thinks I quit. Don't say anything—he's got enough to deal with right now. He was furious when I told him."

"I'm furious, too," Matthew said quietly. "I would've helped you."

"Helped me?" Brianna scoffed. "I haven't even seen you in years." She pulled away, and Matthew instantly missed the feel of her soft skin beneath his fingertips. "Beckett offered to loan me some money, but then he was injured. He couldn't even speak let alone help me out. Believe me when I say I've applied to job after job. Finally, I decided I needed something just to tide me over—to pay the bills. This place sucked, but I was just serving drinks."

Matthew clenched his jaw, trying to control the rage seething inside him. Brianna was far too innocent for her own good. Maybe in her mind she was just serving cocktails in that skimpy little outfit, but to the men frequenting the place? She was the main course.

She was lucky no one had tried anything before tonight. They could've followed her to her car when she left for the evening, followed her home one night. He was actually relieved she was living with her parents. At the very least, she hadn't been returning to an empty apartment at night with God knows who watching.

It made his gut churn just thinking about it, but a pretty woman prancing around like that wouldn't go unnoticed by some men. Her friend Ella was also lucky that nothing had happened to her. God, Brianna had looked fucking spectacular in that skimpy little dress—and to think that other men were admiring her body, watching the way she moved, made him want to inflict bodily harm on any man who'd so much as looked at her the wrong way. Didn't she realize how lucky she was that nothing had happened before tonight?

The squad car in the parking lot suddenly turned on its lights and sirens, causing Brianna to jump. It sped off in another direction, and he and Brianna watched it go. She shivered in the night air, and he grabbed his jacket from where he'd tossed it in the backseat, wrapping it around her shoulders. She was so small and petite. Her head only came up to his shoulder, and his massive jacket completely enveloped her. But he liked seeing her wearing it. Liked feeling like she was his to protect and care for.

"I'll take you home," he said, suddenly feeling unsure. Some asshole had just attacked her in the back hall. Maybe she wanted to curl up in bed in the comfort of her own home and just be left alone. Maybe she needed someone there with her. Hell. What did he know? How he wished he could be the one to hold her—to be there if she woke up crying and scared. To be his to comfort.

"Matthew?" she asked, her voice quiet.

"Yes?"

"Thank you."

Those two little words slayed him. Was she thanking him for earlier? For driving her back right now? It didn't matter. The only thing he needed to worry about was getting her out of here—taking her home and making her feel safe and secure. And he would do whatever it took for that to happen.

# Chapter 9

For the second time in as many days, Brianna fumbled with the lock in her front door, Matthew hovering right behind her. Rather than setting her nerve endings on fire like he had the day before, at the moment, his presence just felt comforting. Reassuring. And some part of her knew that he needed to be there just as much as she needed him right now.

To her surprise, the house was completely dark, with nothing on but the front porch light. A quick glance indicated that her parents' car was gone from the garage, and she stepped inside, puzzled.

"No one's home?" Matthew asked, his voice deep behind her.

"No, that's really strange," she said, flipping on the light switch. "I don't know where they'd go."

"I'll look around," Matthew instructed. "Stay here."

"But—"

"Just let me make sure everything's okay."

Brianna sighed and closed the front door, making sure to lock it behind her. Matthew's arms snaked around her, and he tugged her against his broad chest. "Just humor me, okay?" he asked quietly. He brushed a chaste kiss against her temple, causing her insides to stir.

"Okay," she agreed. Matthew released her, and she dropped her oversized purse down on the floor, sinking into the living room sofa. It was kind of nice to have someone to take care of things for her, she thought. She was so used to being on her own that having Matthew take charge of the situation was actually a relief. In all likelihood, her parents had just decided to pick up some last-minute things to get ready for tomorrow.

"Uh, Bri?" Matthew called out from the kitchen, his voice sounding funny.

She immediately stood and hurried to him. "What's wrong? Did you find something?"

Matthew held a piece of paper in his hand, and she could see her mother's handwriting even from across the room. "My parents left a note? What does it say? Where'd they go?"

"It's about Beckett," Matthew said, his Adam's apple bobbing up and down as he swallowed.

"Oh my God," she said, feeling her heart racing. "Is he okay?"

Matthew cleared his throat, holding the paper out of her reach as she crossed the room toward him. "Bri," he repeated, his green eyes guarded.

"Well give me the note!"

She reached up for it, and Matthew lightly grasped

her wrist. "Beckett's okay." His thumb lightly grazed across her pulse point, and she knew he could tell she was scared.

"But?"

Matthew released her but set the note down on the table behind him, blocking her from it with his large frame. "But he tried to kill himself tonight."

Brianna gasped, covering her mouth with her hands. She sank to the ground as dizziness suddenly overtook her and tears streamed down her cheeks. "What? Why would he do that? He was going to come home! I just talked to him yesterday."

Matthew knelt down beside her, gathering her in his arms. "I don't know," he soothed, letting her cry into his chest for the second time that evening. "Your parents flew up to Walter Reed. Did they try calling you earlier?"

"I don't know; maybe," she gasped. "We're not supposed to have our phones when we're on shift. I didn't even check my messages with everything that happened earlier."

Matthew grunted something in affirmation and rubbed soothing circles on her back as she sobbed against him. He shifted, pulling her closer so that he was cradled her in his lap as they sat on her kitchen floor. A thousand memories of their childhood flooded through her mind—of Matthew coming over to see her and Beckett, of endless summer days spent together. To think that might've never happened again. That the three of them might never stand in the same room together. That her brother had survived a roadside ambush and the loss of one limb but nearly took his own life only one day before he returned home.

Nothing about it made any sense.

"It's better that it happened while he was still there," Matthew said, his voice sad. "At least he's still alive—that they were able to save him. He can get whatever help he needs."

"But the homecoming—everything. Everyone was coming tomorrow. Why would he do that?" she whispered.

"I don't know. The stress from it all, the changes. Guilt that he survived and some other men didn't. That would be tough on anyone."

"It just isn't fair. Hasn't he already been through enough?"

Shakily, Brianna rose to her feet, using one of Matthew's broad shoulders for support. She swiped at the tears on her cheeks, feeling completely defeated. At the moment, she didn't want to think about anything. Anyone.

"Where are you going?" Matthew asked as he stood.

"I don't know. To bed. To take a long shower and wash this day off. I just can't deal with anything else right now."

"Why don't you go shower and change, and I'll make you something to eat. You've had a long day. I don't want you passing out or something."

"Matthew—"

"You're white as a ghost," he said, gently wiping a stray tear away. Somehow even that simple gesture caused a shiver to race down her spine, despite her bone-deep exhaustion. It was crazy how just one touch from Matthew could make everything okay. Could make her yearn for things she had no business wanting or feeling right now.

"All right," she finally agreed. "I'll be back down in a few minutes."

She walked back into the living room to grab her purse as Matthew called out behind her, "Take your time!"

There was something all wrong about having Matthew fix her dinner in her parents' home while she showered upstairs. Something almost boyfriend-like and domestic and completely at odds with who they were to each other. Yet at the same time, it also felt like something completely right.

\*\*\*

Matthew heard the shower running as he opened the refrigerator. Hell, he should call his own parents and tell them what was going on with Beckett and the Millers. Maybe Brianna's parents already had? One thing was for certain—this day sure as shit couldn't get any worse. Thankfully he'd felt the need to escort Brianna inside. What if she'd found that note while she was here all alone? After everything she'd dealt with this evening, she didn't need to go through that by herself. She'd looked so frail a few minutes ago as she'd collapsed on the floor. He'd wanted to pick her up and carry her off to her bedroom right then. And not to make love to her—which he would love to do another time—but just to hold her. Make her feel safe.

His phone buzzed with an incoming text, and Evan's name flashed across the screen.

*That asshole's in jail, but his lawyer is already trying to bail him out.*

Matthew quickly typed a message back.

*Won't they press charges?*

Evan's reply made his stomach clench.

*Dunno.*

Shit. Maybe he could call Patrick tomorrow. His girlfriend, Rebecca, dealt with domestic violence issues in her work as a divorce attorney. She might know how to ensure this guy remained locked up until the trail. Matthew didn't have the first clue as to how to proceed in a situation like this. And he sure the hell didn't feel comfortable in the knowledge that he was leaving tomorrow evening.

The attack on Brianna tonight was most likely a crime of opportunity, but no way was he comfortable leaving until he knew for sure that her attacker was behind bars. He had to get back to his SEAL training in Little Creek, but damn. He'd drag her with him to Virginia Beach if he had to, just to ensure her safety.

It was actually closer to Beckett, too, he reasoned. She could drive up to Walter Reed from there. Maybe he'd talk with her about it tomorrow after things had settled down. They could both visit Beckett on the weekends, offer their support. And as for Brianna staying with him in his little one-bedroom apartment? Well, they'd cross that bridge when they came to it.

He found some ground beef and rolls and decided to cook some burgers on the stove. Now that the adrenaline rush from earlier had worn off, he was starving. And it would do Bri some good to eat something as well. He opened a cupboard, searching for a frying pan, when he heard a loud crash from upstairs. Without even thinking, he bolted across the kitchen, taking the stairs two at a time as he raced up to the home's second level. The bathroom door at the end of the hallway was shut, but he burst inside without even knocking, shouting, "Bri!"

The floral scent of her shampoo filled the steamy bathroom, and he noticed that a towel rack had fallen of the wall and crashed onto the tile floor. But that wasn't what first caught his attention. Brianna had stepped out of the shower looking like some sort of Greek goddess come to life. Damp strands of wavy blonde hair were piled high on her head, her cheeks were flushed from the warm water and steam, and the fluffy towel she was clutching around herself barely concealed her full breasts, which were currently heaving up and down.

"I just—I was just—"

"I'm sorry," he said, attempting to avert his eyes. "I heard the crash and thought you were hurt."

Hell. All parts of his anatomy that shouldn't be responding were ready to stand at full attention at the sight of her. His pants grew tighter, his breathing hitched, and he clenched his fists, willing himself not to go to her. She looked so soft and sweet, so perfectly feminine, that staying completely away became an impossibility. He hastened a glance back to Brianna, where she watched him with wide eyes, her lips slightly parted.

He ran a hand across his stubble, willing himself to get a grip. "I can fix that," he said, gesturing toward the mess on the floor. "I'll clean it up. I mean, after you get undressed. Get dressed," he hastily corrected.

A small smile played about her lips, and Brianna stepped closer to him, raising a delicate hand to his forearm. The feel of her fingertips on his skin was meant to be soothing, but it felt more like a fire was blazing through his veins.

"It's okay," she said softly. "I'm okay."

"Bri, God. I thought something happened….And I didn't mean to barge in here with you looking like…this…." He trailed off, feeling foolish. He knew they were the only two people in the house. What the hell had he expected? He swung his gaze back to her sea green eyes.

"Like what?"

He nailed her with a gaze. "Gorgeous."

She caressed his arm gently, just the barest of touches as her thumb brushed across his heated skin, and something shifted between them. The awful evening they'd spent earlier, the news of her brother, and everything else all faded into the background.

"Matthew," she whispered.

The way she looked up at him was his undoing. At the moment she was gazing at him like he was her whole world. And it felt that way, too. Almost like nothing else existed outside of this room. There was nothing bad, no other people to worry about, just this moment between a man and a woman. Between them.

Brianna loosened her hold on the towel, and his gaze was drawn to her beautiful breasts. They spilled out over the soft material, so full and soft, and suddenly she dropped the towel to the ground, baring herself to him.

"Bri," he murmured, watching the soft peaks rise and fall with each breath she took. Her nipples were pale and gorgeous, like petals against her full globes. He wanted to caress and kiss them, to run his tongue across the pebbled flesh and drive her toward ecstasy.

"I want you, Matthew. I need you."

His lips were on hers in an instant, his hands wrapping around her slender waist, pulling her close.

He tugged her hair free from atop her head, sending blonde waves cascading down. The long strands teased her breasts, falling softly across her skin, and he nearly lost it right there. She was beautiful. Completely perfect. The type of woman that men wrote songs about and sailed across oceans to see. And she was his.

"Make me forget," she whispered as he threaded his hands through her hair and his lips hungrily sought hers. "Make me forget everything."

# Chapter 10

She didn't know where she'd gotten the nerve to go to Matthew. But when he'd burst through the bathroom door, looking so ruggedly handsome while she was practically naked, it had been all she could do not to throw herself at him. Maybe it was the adrenaline from the night's events, the need for something good to come after all the bad that had happened. Maybe it was just the way she'd wanted him for practically a lifetime—but there'd been no stopping the desire surging through her. No resisting him.

Matthew bent and lifted her into his arms, carrying her down the hall toward her bedroom as if she weighed nothing at all. He laid her atop the bed like she was something delicate and fragile, something to be cherished and adored. Matthew leaned over and pressed a searing kiss on her lips and then stood and pulled his shirt from his pants. He tugged it off over his head, revealing tanned, smooth flesh that stretched across his rippling muscles. Broad pectorals gave way to chiseled abs and a perfect "v" of muscles that led down toward his trousers. She could see the bulge in them even now. He reached for his belt but then stopped and just stared at her, his green eyes blazing.

His eyes raked over her, taking in every curve, lingering on her breasts and swollen sex. Suddenly she felt self-conscious and raised her hands to cover herself. Although she was curvy and toned, Matthew was male perfection. She didn't need him examining every square inch of her.

"Don't hide from me," he quietly commanded. "Never hide from me."

He lightly grabbed her wrists and pulled her arms away, drinking in the sight of her naked form as she trembled beneath his gaze. Gently holding her wrists, he ducked down, his hot breath on her skin before he kissed and teased one nipple. She arched off the bed and cried out, the sensations of Matthew's mouth and tongue on her overwhelming. He kissed around one areola, leaving her whimpering for more as he took his sweet time. At last Mathew flicked her nipple gently with his tongue, causing her to moan beneath him. His hand sought her other breast, and soon he was lightly squeezing and caressing.

His touch was so soft, it was almost impossible to believe that a man so big could be so gentle. His thumb skimmed across her pert nipple, and as he lightly pinched it, she gasped.

"Matthew," she panted, arching toward him again as he sucked one nipple into his mouth. He was relentless, teasing her and building her up until she felt every sensation in her core. Her sex became swollen, dripping with arousal, and as Matthew trailed a large hand down the side of her body, she knew he'd find her wet and ready for him. He teased her for a moment, his knuckles lightly grazing her mound, and she bucked beneath him. Finally, his fingers delved through her tender folds, parting her to him, and slipped through her silken arousal.

She gasped as he explored her, his touch soft and tender. Her entire body felt like it might explode just from his gentle caresses. At last he moved his fingers higher and slowly circled her clit, causing her to cry out as pleasure surged through her.

He continued suckling her breasts as his adept fingers slowly drove her toward the precipice. Warmth coiled down from her belly, surging out from her center and setting her entire body alight from his touch.

She'd never felt this way with a man before, never had someone so completely control and command her body. Helplessly, she whimpered for more, wanting and needed him to drive her over the edge. Matthew finally slid two thick fingers into her swollen channel, stretching and readying her for him. Her inner walls clenched down around him, and as his thumb rubbed over her clit, she cried out again, feeling the waves of pleasure beginning to overtake her.

He circled around and around her sensitive bud, building her up as his fingers thrust in and out, filling her. She began to see stars as he increased the pace, and suddenly she was screaming out in pleasure as her orgasm went on and on.

Matthew slowly eased her back down from

heaven, and as she lay gasping on the bed, he quickly shucked his pants and boxer briefs. His thick erection sprang free, and he covered her body with his, kissing her softly as his arousal rubbed against her thigh. It was thick and heavy, and she wrapped her fingers around his impressive length, stroking him gently. Matthew deepened their kiss, his tongue parting her lips and plunging into her mouth. His massive erection jerked in her hand, and Matthew pulled back slightly, a lazy grin spreading across his face.

"Go easy on me, love. You're my every fantasy come to life."

He reached for his discarded pants and pulled a foil packet from his wallet, quickly sheathing himself before he nudged her legs apart with his knee. Her legs fell open as he knelt before her, and his thick arms landed on either side of her head as he ducked lower and kissed her neck.

Trailing soft kisses from beneath her earlobe down to her collarbone, he teased and nipped at her. She tilted her head back, allowing him greater access, and tried to shift beneath him as she felt his erection prodding against her entrance. His muscular body hovered above her, teasing and tempting her as he took his time. She needed to feel him filling her up, claiming her, easing the ache that was once again building inside.

His teeth grazed across the sensitive skin of her neck and as she cried out and arched up to him, he finally shifted positions, slowly penetrating her throbbing center with his swollen head.

She gasped at the exquisite pressure as his engorged shaft stretched and filled her completely. He was perfect, as if made just for her. His thick cock throbbed as her inner walls pulsed around him, and when he was seated completely inside her, he stilled for a moment, letting her get used to the intimate invasion. She gasped beneath him, pinned beneath his large body, completely at his mercy. *Matthew* was making love to her, kissing her, filling her with his hard length. His green eyes met hers, and she was shocked at the depth of love and emotion she saw in them.

He slowly withdrew and thrust gently in once more, stroking her inner walls. She cried out as the base of his penis rubbed against her still swollen clit, and he ground against her, causing her to see stars. Matthew grasped her hands, lacing their fingers together, and raised them above her head. She wanted to touch him, to feel his solid muscles beneath her fingertips, but he held her in place, completely at his mercy. Matthew was the type of man used to commanding and controlling the situation, and it seemed he was determined to take charge in the bedroom as well.

He began thrusting harder as she whimpered and writhed beneath him, her legs spread wide, her body his for the taking. His muscular chest rubbed against her sensitive nipples with every stroke, and shockwaves of pleasure began to rock through her again.

Each deep thrust sent her closer to another Earth-shattering orgasm. She'd never come during sex before, but with Matthew, it seemed inevitable. Helplessly she surrendered to him, letting him take her body to soaring new heights. Warmth surged through her, and she couldn't hold back the start of her orgasm.

"Matthew, oh God!" she cried out.

"Come for me, Brianna."

His gruff command left her gasping.

She wrapped her legs around his waist, desperate to have him as close as possible. To have him push her over the edge. His hips bucked relentlessly, pounding into her wet heat. She desperately clutched onto his hands, hanging on for dear life as he sought her pleasure. Heat surged through her entire body, and Matthew ducked down and kissed her, stealing her breath, and swallowing her cries. Her orgasm bloomed out of nowhere as Matthew thrust deeper, and she cried out his name as an intense tsunami of pleasure overtook her, drawing her under and drowning all her senses.

Her screams went on and on, and she lost count of how many times he made her come around him. She'd never climaxed so many times or so hard before, and finally she lay breathless beneath him, at a loss for all words. Matthew pulled out, and before she could ask what was happening, he flipped her over, positioning her hips and entering her from behind. She cried out once more in pleasure as he filled her swollen channel, and he felt impossibly bigger in the position. His hands found her breasts, and he cupped and massaged them as he chased down his own release.

Brianna gripped onto the sheets as his thick length filled her again and again, impossibly stirring the beginnings of another orgasm inside her. Her inner walls clenched around him as she gasped with pleasure, Matthew slid one hand beneath her, finding her clit. As his fingers caressed her throbbing nub, she came again, screaming as he drove into her.

Matthew stiffened, his cock growing impossibly harder, and gave two more solid thrusts as he finally released deep inside her sex.

She collapsed, her head resting against the soft sheets, as Matthew ducked down and kissed her bare shoulder, breathing heavily. A light sheen of sweat coated both their bodies, and they remained that way a moment, Matthew's body covering hers, still intimately joined together.

Matthew finally pulled out and rolled to the side, pulling her with him. He held her securely in his arms and brushed a tender kiss to her temple as she melted into his embrace.

"Holy hell, Bri," he finally said, his voice still thick with desire. "That was…wow." His hand slid to her breast, cupping it possessively as he wrapped his large frame around her, drawing her closer still.

"That's an understatement."

His hands slid over her body, gently caressing, as if he couldn't stop touching her.

She felt him growing hard again behind her, and his fingers slid to her clit, readying her again for him. He leaned over and lightly bit down on her earlobe as he teased her sensitive bundle of nerves, and she felt dizzy with lust and desire. It seemed impossible to want him again so soon, but her body was already craving his touch, his kisses, and aching for him to fill her once more.

"I want to make love to you all night," he said gruffly, sliding two fingers inside her molten core.

"Yes," she whispered, already bucking lightly against his hand. He withdrew his fingers, and she rolled over to face him in the darkness, hitching one leg up over his as he drew her close. His lips hungrily sought hers, erasing all thoughts, stealing her breath, and she was once again lost only to him.

# Chapter 11

Matthew awoke with a start the next morning, squinting at his surroundings as sunlight peeked in through the blinds. Memories of the night before suddenly came flooding back as Brianna shifted in his arms. Her breasts brushed against his forearms as he held her to him, and his erection thickened against her bare ass.

She was curvy and gorgeous and fit perfectly in his arms as if she'd been made for him and him alone. He'd never dared hope he'd hold Brianna before, let alone spend the night exploring her body, pleasuring her, and learning what she liked.

Taking her from behind after they'd first made love the night before had made him harder than steel. Her pussy had clamped down so tightly on his cock that he'd thought he'd explode the second he'd entered her. His hands itched to knead and massage her full breasts again. Someday he wanted to have her riding him—watching those breasts bounce up and down as he bucked beneath her, making her come atop his cock.

His eyes fell on the nightstand, where a message light flashed on his phone.

Hell.

Recollections of the day before suddenly ruined his good mood. The creep who'd attacked Brianna at the cocktail lounge. The news of Beckett attempting to take his own life. The world was falling to pieces around him, and he'd been so lost in Brianna he'd forgotten about everything else for eight hours.

Guilt seeped through him as he thought of his best friend. On what was probably one of the worst days of Beckett's life, Matthew had screwed his sister. Not that Brianna was just some one-night-stand to him. But hell. He had no right to spend the night in her bed.

He edged up onto one elbow, trying not to wake Bri, and reached across her for his phone. Her bare breasts spilled out above the tousled sheets and rose and fell softly with each breath she took. His breath caught as his cock rose to attention. Damn. He could spend all day gazing at her, touching her soft skin, kissing and caressing her everywhere. Pleasuring her in every way imaginable.

He had no right to want her that way—no claim to her. Hell, he was supposed to be leaving in twelve hours. And even though she'd come onto him last night, baring herself to him in the bathroom, after what she'd been through? He probably should've tucked her in bed and went on his merry way.

He eased away from her sleeping form, sitting up as he swung his legs down to the floor. Her panties were tossed onto the ground along with his pants and other discarded clothing. His gut clenched—something just felt so right about being there with Brianna. How could he go on with his life acting like nothing had changed between them?

He swiped the screen on his phone, seeing Evan's message asking what time Beckett was arriving.

Hell.

He needed to call his buddies and let them know what was happening. That the entire thing was off. It was damn early though. He quickly sent off a text message to Evan and Brent, giving only the barest of details. He'd fill them in more after he'd had coffee and food. Snagging his boxers and pants from the floor, he pulled them on, heading downstairs to Brianna's kitchen.

His own childhood home was his view out the kitchen window, and he tried not to laugh at the irony of his situation—of falling for the girl next door. It had only taken what—a lifetime to end up in her bed? But something inside him craved a whole lot more than one night.

He opened the cupboards and finally pulled out coffee and two mugs. A few minutes later coffee was brewing, and he debated fixing her breakfast. They'd never gotten around to eating dinner last night, and his empty stomach rumbled.

"Matthew?"

Brianna's sleepy form appeared in the doorway, wearing only a silk robe that he longed to unwrap. Her blonde waves were sexy and tousled, like she'd spent the night being thoroughly ravished. His heart clenched, and he crossed the room to her, consequences be damned. So what if they had only one day together before he had to fly home. So what if they couldn't ever be anything real. He would make the most of the moment. Yesterday she'd asked him to make her forget, and if that's what she wanted, he'd damn well do it.

Matthew cupped her face in his hands and ducked down and kissed her softly. She stretched up on her tiptoes and wound her arms round his neck. He could feel the softness of her breasts pushing against his bare chest, and the silkiness of her robe sliding across his skin felt like the barest of caresses. His hands fumbled with the sash, untying it, and then her robe was falling open, baring her to him.

The soft material curtained her full breasts, giving him a glorious view of her full globes, petal pink nipples, and trim pussy down below. He palmed her breasts, running his thumbs across her nipples in the way that she liked, and a pleased smile tugged at his lips as she unwittingly arched into him. He nipped at her neck, kissing his way down her body. Briefly, he laved her breasts with his tongue before kissing his way down her flat stomach as she trembled. He could smell the scent of her arousal, and his cock instantly hardened.

Later.

This was about her pleasure right now.

He easily lifted one of Brianna's slender legs over his shoulder as she gasped.

"Matthew, wait. What—?"

She moaned as he parted her folds with his thumbs and gave one hard lick up her seam. She tasted amazing, like the sweetest of all nectars. He could drink her sweet release all day and die a happy man. Her hand fell to his shoulder, seeking balance, and he kissed her core, listening to her little gasps of pleasure as he lapped up her juices. "Matthew, no one's ever…."

He paused for a moment and looked up to her flushed face. She looked so gorgeous standing in front of him—so vulnerable and beautiful and completely his in that moment. Her soft waves fell to her full breasts, making her look like an angel sent down from heaven just for him. An angel he wanted to worship and pleasure where no man ever had before.

"I love that I'm the first man to ever taste you," he said, his voice gravel. "To give you pleasure like this."

"Matthew," she whimpered.

"I'll take care of you, darlin'."

He kissed her again, laving through her delicate folds with his tongue. Her sex quivered against his lips, and he felt a surge of male pride that she'd given herself over to him like this. He lightly licked her clit as she gasped, and he teased her with light ministrations. She clutched his head, holding him to her, and he wanted to beat his chest in approval. Gripping her curvy hip as he held her in place, he slid two fingers into her tight channel, feeling her velvety walls clench down around him.

Brianna cried out and nearly came undone. He suckled her clit, pleasuring her as he slowly worked his fingers in and out. He could tell she was close as her breathing grew heavy, and he increased his tempo, laving her again and again with his tongue until she screamed out his name.

Heat bloomed within his chest at taking her pleasure. She was panting and gasping, her leg hooked over his shoulder, her swollen sex still fluttering against his mouth. He kissed her softly then lifted her leg down, pulling her down into his lap. She curled against him, breathless, nestling her head into the crook of his shoulder.

"I could go down on you all day," he muttered, and Brianna shivered in his arms. "You taste so damn amazing."

"Wow," she murmured breathlessly. "That was—wow."

"I love that you let me do that for you," he said, running his fingers through her blonde waves. They fell to her breasts, only partially covered by her silky robe.

Hell. He loved that she'd come for him like that. How on Earth was he supposed to let her go after a moment like that?

He couldn't.

Wouldn't.

His phone buzzed on the counter, and he blew out a breath he didn't even realize he'd been holding. One of the guys had probably gotten his text about Beckett. They'd all fly out tonight as originally planned, just without attending the homecoming ceremony on base today. He had exactly one day to spend with the woman of his dreams. And his gut churned with the knowledge that one day would never be enough.

# Chapter 12

Brianna tossed her sunscreen into her beach tote an hour later and looked around her room for a sun hat. The past twenty-four hours had been completely surreal. There'd been her shift at the cocktail lounge where she'd spotted Matthew, being accosted in the hallway by a drunken idiot, learning of her brother's attempt at taking his own life, and then somehow ending up spending the night with Matthew in her bed. In the span of a day she'd gone through both heaven and hell.

She flushed, recalling all the ways Matthew had taken her. He'd made her come so many times, she didn't think she'd ever be the same again. Having him flip her over and thrust into her from behind as he'd massaged her breasts had been exciting and sexy as hell. He'd been in complete control, commanding her body to reach unimaginable new heights. She'd never felt so powerless yet so desired and completely worshiped at the same time. No man could compare to the way he'd given her pleasure, and the sweet, gentle kisses that had gone along with all the mind-blowing orgasms had nearly made her come undone. Unbelievably, the reality of being with Matthew far surpassed the fantasy.

After kissing her intimately in the kitchen this morning—something no man had ever done before—he'd fixed them both breakfast, insisting she sit down and enjoy her coffee. She'd been so flushed and thoroughly satisfied that she could hardly move, let alone insist that she help him. She could get used to watching him move shirtless around the kitchen in the morning, flipping pancakes and grinning from ear-to-ear as they had breakfast together. And since he had the day here before his flight took off from base later this evening, and her parents had convinced her to stay home and not fly up to Walter Reed to see Beckett, Matthew had somehow talked her into going snorkeling with him.

A day alone with him seemed almost reckless—especially when she knew she'd only fall harder. Matthew had just told her the other night he wouldn't ever be in a serious relationship or marry. This was probably just a fling to him—one in an endless string he no doubt had over the years. Was it too much to hope that she'd somehow change his mind? He was a first-class flirt and a single, eligible SEAL. Of course women would fall at his feet. She'd been in love with him practically forever, but she had a feeling that after today, she'd be in way too deep.

How could she say no to spending a day alone with him though? This was her only chance. The next time they saw one another, Beckett would be back, and everything would change. They'd be buddies again, friends and not lovers…or whatever it was they were at the moment.

Her phone buzzed from inside her tote bag, and she saw Ella's name flash across the screen as she grabbed it.

"Hey Ella."

"Hi! How are you? I just wanted to make sure you were okay after last night."

"Yeah, I'm okay. Thanks for checking up on me. Last night was awful, but Matthew brought me home and stayed with me a while. Did you get home okay after dropping the other guys off?"

"Yeah, it was nice to have the company since I was a little freaked out when we left. That one guy Brent is a bit much, but Evan seemed nice. He was telling me how his girlfriend's pregnant and everything. I think he knew I was pretty overwhelmed."

"God, I am never going back there," Brianna groaned. "Just the idea of setting foot in the building makes me sick."

"Do you know what's going to happen to the guy who attacked you?"

"The police called earlier. They're pressing charges and holding him until the trial—everything's on video, so his lawyer couldn't get him out on bail." She cringed, thinking about other people watching the footage. She'd been so scared and helpless when that stranger had pinned her against the wall, intending to have his wicked way with her. To grope her, rape her. God, if Matthew hadn't been there—tears filled her eyes just thinking about it.

"Well that's good news, I guess. I mean, not good that it happened, but that the guy is in jail for now.

We won't have to worry about running into him somewhere."

Brianna blew out a sigh and wiped a stray tear away. "It was a crazy night. I wish I could just forget that it ever happened. I wish that it *hadn't* happened."

"Frank actually left a message on my cell earlier," Ella admitted.

"What? Why? Was he calling to apologize or something?"

Ella let out a bitter laugh. "Hell no. He called to try to pressure me into coming back. He understands why you're not—and I think he's scared of all those guys you were with."

"I don't even know them aside from Matthew."

"Would you believe that jerk didn't even mention you in his message? He just wanted me to come in. I haven't called him back yet, but there's no way I can keep working there."

"You'll find something else. I know we both hated it before, but now? I just don't think it's safe. There's no security, no one to stop a customer from doing whatever they want."

"I know. Don't worry; I have no plans to work there again. Ever. But I was also calling because I got your text earlier. Your brother's not coming home today?"

"No," Brianna said with a sigh. "There were some, uh, complications. Maybe we can meet tomorrow and chat? I just don't even want to go into it right now."

"Yeah, sure. You must be pretty disappointed he can't make it home yet. I've got classes all morning but am free after that."

"Tomorrow afternoon is fine. I just really don't want to get into it over the phone."

"All right. You can fill me in tomorrow. Let me know if you need anything."

"Will do. Let's chat tomorrow and figure out a time to meet up."

They said their goodbyes, and Brianna finished packing her tote bag. That was strange that Frank had tried to persuade Ella to return to work. It bothered her that he was contacting Ella at all now that she'd quit. If he called her again, she'd tell the man off herself. Ella didn't need any trouble and sure didn't have to put up with his crap anymore.

The doorbell rang, and Brianna glanced at her clock, realizing that Matthew was already here. She hadn't even been snorkeling in years, but Matthew was a Navy SEAL for heaven's sake. Certainly he knew how to SCUBA dive and could teach her the snorkeling basics she'd long since forgotten. She just hoped she didn't make a fool of herself in front of him. Not that it mattered much anyway. After today he'd be flying home, and who knew when he'd ever be back.

She tried to ignore the ache in her heart at the thought of not seeing him again for a while. She hurried to the front door and pulled it open. Matthew stood on her front porch in navy blue swim trunks and an old tee shirt, aviators shading his eyes. "Hey," he said as she looked up at him.

"Hi. Is everything okay? You look really serious."

"Yeah, it's just—can we talk for a minute before we head out?"

"Uh, sure."

Brianna's heart pounded in her chest, and she wondered if he was about to drop a bombshell on her. After everything that had happened, she wasn't sure she could deal with more bad news.

"Let's go sit down," he said, perching his aviators atop of his head. He rested a hand on the small of her back to guide her toward the sofa in the living room. She sat down, nervously placing her hands in her lap, and Matthew paced in front of her, sucking far too much oxygen from out of the room. Her heart pounded, and she took a gulp of air. Maybe something had happened to Beckett? Why else would he be acting so strangely?

"Did something happen?" she finally blurted out.

Matthew turned and gazed at her with bright green eyes. He'd shaved since this morning, and his chiseled features looked even more pronounced without the whiskers covering his jaw. "Bri, I'm feeling guilty as hell about what happened last night. Don't get me wrong—I loved every minute of it, but you were upset. I shouldn't have taken advantage of you like that."

Relief washed over her, and she stood, crossing over to him. "God, you scared me. I thought Beckett was—" she cut off, unwilling to even finish the thought.

"Shit. I'm sorry, I didn't mean to frighten you. I just needed to apologize—I should've watched out for you better last night, not taken advantage of the situation."

"That's what you think happened?"

He ran a hand across his jaw, looking pained. "That guy attacked you in the bar. And when we got back to your place, instead of fixing you dinner and telling you goodnight, I spent the entire night in your bed. And hell, it was amazing. Fucking fantastic. But that doesn't make it right."

Hurt seeped through her. Matthew knew as well as she did that she was the one who had initiated things yesterday. For God's sake, she'd basically stripped for him in the bathroom. Maybe he thought he was letting her down easy and this was just his way of telling her he didn't want to be with her. Of course she already realized that—he was leaving tonight. He might have spent the night with her, but she'd known it wouldn't be something long term. Still, she expected that things would just fizzle out when he was gone—not that he'd reject her mere hours after leaving her house.

She tried to blink away the tears in her eyes before he noticed them. Even if he had hurt her, she sure the hell wasn't going to let him know it. Maybe she'd cry into her pillow later on, but there was no way she was giving him the satisfaction. "Look, don't worry about it."

He nodded, looking uncertain.

"If you have stuff to do, we don't have to go snorkeling today. But I could use a ride to pick up my car."

Relief washed over his features. "We can go snorkeling if you like. But we can't—nothing can happen between us again."

"Right," she agreed, planting a fake smile on face. "That's probably for the best." She turned and crossed back to the foyer, grabbing her beach tote. Matthew's rejection stung, but there was no way she was going to let him see it. They'd spend a few hours together, she'd show him what he was missing, and then he'd be gone. Which was always going to be the ending to the weekend.

So why did it have to hurt so damn much?

# Chapter 13

Matthew tried to look away as Brianna slipped off her beach cover-up half an hour later, revealing a red string bikini.

Hell.

*That's* what she was wearing snorkeling today?

The top barely covered her full breasts, which were prominently on display as she bent over to retrieve her sunscreen from the sand. The skimpy bottoms were tied with red bows at her curvy hips, and the tiny patch of fabric barely covered that sweet spot he'd sunk into last night and finally tasted this morning. Straight blonde hair fell past her shoulders, and when she stood back up, she pulled it into some kind of twist atop her head, her breasts rising with the movement.

He looked out at the ocean, his groin tightening, and pulled his shirt from over his head.

He'd felt nothing but guilty since leaving after

breakfast this morning. As soon as he'd walked back over to his parents' house it had been a crash back into reality. He'd had to tell his parents the news about Beckett, confirm his ride out of here tonight, and be ready for training bright and early in the morning. He had half a mind to cancel on Brianna completely, avoiding temptation. But hell. He cared about her. And that was why he'd had to apologize and let her know that taking things to the next level had been a colossal mistake.

A light breeze blew in off the water, and it was a crystal clear day, as perfect as they come. The chance of a rainstorm later this afternoon was slim, but he figured they'd be finished snorkeling long before then anyway. And after that, he'd be packing his things to get the hell out of dodge. He'd dreaded coming home for weeks—dreaded facing his best friend. Now an entire new host of worries churned through him: Brianna's safety when she was out. Beckett's recovery from his suicide attempt.

Lots of men and women in the military ended up with PTSD, and that could mess with your mind. Or he could have been depressed at the loss of his limb or in too much pain. Once Matthew got settled back in at Little Creek he'd make a trip up to Walter Reed. If his buddy needed his support, he'd be there. Every damn weekend if he had to be.

Funny that now he dreaded leaving town when less than forty-eight hours ago he couldn't wait to get the hell out of here. His entire life had been rocked to the core after everything with Brianna—witnessing the man attacking her at the bar, feeling like his heart was being ripped out as she cried in fear, and then ending up spending the night with her safe in his arms. Almost as if it was right where she belonged. The weekend had been a whirlwind of emotions, and he didn't know how else to leave but to let her know that they were better off just being friends. What else could he do? He had to return to Little Creek. He deployed all the time. And breaking up would hurt a hell of a lot more later.

He eyed the reef out in the distance, hoping Brianna would be okay to swim out there with her snorkeling gear. Maybe he should've rented a boat, but he'd been flying by the seat of his pants ever since first spotting Bri at the bar last night. Hell, he barely knew up from down at the moment with the chaotic thoughts churning through his head.

He walked back over to where Brianna was currently smoothing sunscreen down her arms. God damn she was beautiful. And he shouldn't even touch her.

He cleared his throat, and she glanced over at him, her mouth slightly parting. He couldn't see her eyes from behind the oversized sunglasses she wore, but he had a feeling she was upset. Whether with him, her brother, or the asshole from last night, he wasn't entirely sure. She'd sure the hell seemed happy this morning, despite the circumstances. After their brief chat in her living room a little while ago though, she'd been distant and aloof. Which meant all signs pointed to him.

The trouble was, everything he wanted to do to fix it, to make it up to her, was impossible.

"I meant to tell you, I called the police station earlier," he said, his voice gruff.

"You did? They called me this morning."

Matthew stiffened. "What did they say?"

"Just that they're holding him until the trail. They have, uh, footage of the incident." She looked away from him, back out at the water, biting her lower lip. Matthew longed to skim his thumb across it. To pull her into his arms and kiss away all the unhappiness she was feeling. To make her forget, as she'd begged him last night.

"You didn't say anything. I was worried they'd let that asshole out on bail."

Brianna shrugged. "They called half an hour before you came over. I figured I'd tell you then, but you wanted to talk...."

Matthew nodded. Some jerk he was. Had he even asked her how she was feeling this morning? He'd been so hell-bent on hearing her cry out his name again as he made her come, on tasting the sweetness of her swollen flesh, that he hadn't bothered to check on her actual well-being. It was a dick move, and he knew it.

"I'm glad that jerk's in jail. I was worried about leaving town if he was out on bail."

"I don't work there anymore. It's not like he can find me. It was just being in the wrong place at the wrong time."

"I still wish I wasn't so far away. Beckett's not here, and I'm based up in Little Creek. I'd have to catch a flight just to get down here."

"We both knew you were leaving tonight. Don't make a bigger deal out of it than it is." She turned and picked up the snorkeling gear they'd rented, but he could hear the hurt in her voice. Had spending the night with him hurt her? Or just his bumbled apology saying it had all been a mistake?

"Bri...."

"Should we go snorkeling or what?" she asked, refusing to meet his gaze. "You have to leave later on. I have to—well, find a job for starters. Call my parents again to check on Beckett. Deal with the police and whatever comes from that. Look for an apartment. I have enough to worry about."

*Without you.*

Matthew blew out a sigh. He deserved her coldness. Hell, he deserved a lot worse than that. "The reef's way out there," he said, pointing to where some people stood in the distance. "Are you okay to swim out that far with our gear?"

Brianna glanced out to where he was pointing, a look of hesitation crossing over her face.

"We don't have to go. I should've rented a boat for us to go snorkeling today."

"No, I'll be fine."

"You sure?" he asked, raising his eyebrows.

Brianna rolled her eyes. "Look, I'm not a freaking Navy SEAL, but I can swim, Matthew. We grew up together, remember? Spent every summer out on the water?"

"I care about you," he said, hating that she stood a few feet away from him. She belonged in his arms, not off to the side suddenly looking distant and cold. He'd done that though—he'd been the one to put a wall between them when he showed up at her door earlier. They shouldn't have crossed the line in the first place, but now that they had, was he wrong to pretend nothing had changed? To try to go back to how things used to be between them?

"Yeah, I get that. We're friends, remember?"

"I'm sorry about before. About everything."

"You said that already. Let's go before we run out

136

of time. You're leaving in a few hours." She turned and stalked off toward the water, if a woman could do that in a skimpy bikini. Her hips swished back and forth, and it was all he could do not to claim her again right there. To kiss her and caress her, to haul her back home and make love to her all day. To go AWOL and miss his damn flight home tonight.

His gut churned as he grabbed his gear and hustled after Brianna. He'd already made enough mistakes this weekend. He sure the hell didn't need to add one more to his list. Maybe he'd hurt her, but it would hurt a hell of a lot worse when he wasn't around. If they were together but she was always waiting, wondering where he was and when he'd return, she'd understand. It was better to break things off now before they really got started. To go back to being friends.

The only trouble was, he wasn't sure if he could manage that.

*\*\*\**

Brianna muttered under her breath as she tripped over her flippers in the shallow water and ungracefully fell over with a splash. The school of fish scattered in the clear, turquoise waters, and she tried to remember why she'd enjoyed this when she was younger. Or why she'd agreed to go snorkeling with Matthew today.

She was supposed to be celebrating her brother's long-awaited homecoming, spending the day with family, not out here making a fool of herself. She didn't even have her phone with her in case her parents needed to reach her or someone else contacted her from the police station. She supposed that Matthew had thought this would be a fun distraction from what was going on at the moment, but her mind was on everything but the fish she was supposed to be admiring.

Chunks of shells cut against her hands as she struggled to push herself back up, and a strand of hair fell into her face. Maybe flippers were good for swimming, but they were pretty lousy for attempting to walk around in. No one else seemed to be having as much trouble as her though.

She lost her footing again as she tried to stand, dropping her goggles and snorkel into the water, which she'd long since pulled from her face.

"I got you," a deep voice said, and suddenly Matthew's strong hands were wrapping around her waist, lifting her back onto her feet. He held her directly in front of him, his chest to her back, and the feel of his fingers against her bare flesh sent tingles rushing down her arms and warmth coiling in her belly. She froze, not daring to move.

"Are you okay?"

"Fine," she said stiffly, pulling his hands from her waist and awkwardly turning to face him. Droplets of water ran down his bronzed skin, and she tried not to stare at his wall of muscles. At those wide shoulders, broad pecs, and eight-pack abs. Or into those deep green eyes. Jesus Christ. The man had been inside her last night, and now he was just standing there acting like everything was fine and it was cool that they were back to being just friends. He'd barely even spoken to her since they'd made it out to the reef aside from giving her a few brief instructions on snorkeling.

Which hadn't helped, since she kept tripping in the

damn flippers.

It almost felt like the awkward morning-after talk had been postponed until this afternoon. Except instead of one of them sneaking away at the break of dawn, they'd decided to spend the day together. And it wouldn't have been miserable if he hadn't insisting on drawing the line on where things stood between them. On reminding her that he was the man she could never be with. She never should have come to the beach with him after that little chat. If anything, she should have shown him the door. Maybe he hadn't been taking advantage of her, but after that conversation? She felt even worse than she had last night.

Glancing over, she watched her mask and snorkel bobbing up and down beside her. She'd had just about enough of this day.

Matthew snagged her mask from the water as a young couple near them happily splashed around, snapping pictures with a waterproof camera. As they stood back up, laughing, Brianna burst into tears.

"Hey," Matthew said, stepping closer. He cupped her cheek with one hand and brushed the tears away with his thumb. "Don't cry."

"Let's just call it a day," Brianna said miserably.

"You want me to take you home?"

"Yeah, let's just go," she said, her voice cracking. "I want to go home."

"Why are you crying?" he asked gently.

She looked up at him helplessly through watery eyes. "I just—this just wasn't a good idea."

"I care about you. I'm sorry for botching things up earlier, but I'd never want to hurt you."

"You have a strange way of showing it," she

whispered.

Matthew's eyes blazed, and then suddenly he ducked down and kissed her, stealing her breath. His hot lips moved over her mouth like a man starved, and his hands pulled her closer. She tasted the saltiness of her tears and a hint of mint and musk that was pure Matthew. His hands moved to her waist, a second later he was hauling her up into his arms. Her ill-fitting flippers slid off, and she wrapped her legs around him, feeling the thick length of his erection right at her core. She gasped as he held her against him, his arms snaring so tightly around her, she was sure this time he'd never let her go.

"I'm taking you home," he said between kisses, his voice gravel. "And making love to you for the rest of the afternoon. I thought I should stay away from you, but I just can't."

"Yes," she whimpered, letting his tongue penetrate her mouth and sweep inside. He thrust into her mouth slowly, letting her know exactly what he wished they were doing right now. She didn't even care if other people were watching, she needed Matthew as much as she needed her next breath.

He supported her weight with one muscular forearm and snagged her flippers from the water's surface. In an instant, he'd turned and was walking them back the way they'd come earlier as if he did that sort of thing every day. Maybe he did. She didn't care about anything else as the water lapped around her and Matthew held her securely against his hard body. He strode onto the shore a few minutes later, kicking his flippers off when they passed the water line.

"I can stand," she gasped between kisses.

"I like holding you close."

He dropped their snorkeling apparatus onto the sand and kept moving until they reached their discarded towels and beach gear. Swiping both towels from the sand, he carried her off toward some hidden dunes.

"Do you trust me?" he asked.

"Yes, but what are we—?"

His mouth was on hers again in an instant, and he gripped her body, slowly rubbing her against his throbbing erection.

"Oh!" she gasped as heat bloomed inside her. She'd been growing steadily more aroused from the moment he'd first kissed her, but to have him handle her this way would surely drive her completely out of her mind.

Matthew only stopped when they were hidden from view, and he set her down for a moment to spread their towels down on the soft sand. "I can't wait until we get back," he growled, pulling her toward him again. His hands fumbled with the ties of her red bikini top, and soon the triangle cups were falling forward, baring her to him.

"So beautiful," he murmured, laying her down on a towel. He palmed her breasts with his hands, caressing them gently as he nibbled on the tender flesh of her neck. She cried out and arched toward him, arousal dampening her bikini bottoms. His teeth skimmed across her flesh, and then he kissed his way south, moving down the slope of one breast. He sucked a taut bud into his mouth, worshiping her, teasing her. His thumb ran across her other nipple, leaving her writhing beneath him.

"Please, Matthew, I need more."

He flicked his tongue lightly over her peaked nipple, and she cried out, thankful for the loud waves crashing against the shore. His knuckles skimmed across her stomach, and then he kissed his way down from her breasts, moving tenderly down her abdomen. He tugged the flimsy strings of her bikini bottom, yanking it free, and she was exposed to him. Matthew ducked down, lifting her legs over his broad shoulders, opening her completely to him. He lapped at her, drinking in her arousal as she whimpered and clutched onto the towel for dear life. Heat coiled down from her belly, spreading warmth through her entire body.

She felt like she was floating away, unable to do anything but yield to the pleasure he was giving her. His broad shoulders spread her legs wide, and she couldn't move away from the intensity that was pure Matthew. He lightly teased her clit with soft ministrations, and she nearly cried at the sweet pleasure of it all. Without warning he increased his pace, leaving her helplessly bucking against his mouth as she gasped. Matthew's hands slid beneath her bare bottom, and suddenly he lifted her toward him, like she was the feast he was devouring.

Brianna cried out as he lapped at her, unable to move away. He trailed his tongue through all of her sensitive folds and finally penetrated her with his tongue, pulsing in and out of her channel as she moaned out his name. She was so far gone she didn't even care what she sounded like. Matthew finally sucked her clit into his mouth, lightly grazing his teeth across the sensitive bud, and suddenly she screamed as the onslaught of pleasure overtook her. Matthew didn't let up, holding her to him as her orgasm went on and on, and he lapped at her and drank all of her release.

She lay gasping as he moved over her, his chest brushing against her tender nipples. Matthew tugged his swim trunks partway down, and she felt his thick length nudging at her core. She edged her hand down, wrapping her fingers around him, feeling the heavy weight of him in her palm, the velvety softness surrounding steel. Matthew groaned as his cock jerked in her hand. She guided him to her entrance, and then he thrust in, making her his once more.

Her walls clamped down around him, milking him as the aftershocks of her orgasm coursed through her. He slowly withdrew and thrust back in, his face clenched as he tried to hold himself back.

"Faster," she breathed, wrapping her legs around his hips.

His thick length speared her again and again as he increased the pace of his thrusts, and she moaned in pleasure as he penetrated and filled her completely. Matthew rubbed her clit with his thumb and pumped into her, relentless, unyielding, until she threw her head back in ecstasy. He came right along with her, stiffening inside her and softly muttering her name like an oath.

Matthew panted into her neck, alternately kissing and nuzzling her. Brianna lay dazed beneath him, loving the feel of the weight of his body atop hers. He had her completely beneath him, thoroughly sated. His semi-hard cock still twitched inside her, and as he pulled free, she realized they'd forgotten to put on a condom in their haste. She did a quick calculation in her head, deeming it unlikely that she'd actually have anything to worry about from one episode of careless behavior. Hell, it had been worth it.

"Shit," Matthew muttered, apparently having the same thought as her. "Condom."

"I think we're okay. I mean, I'm not on birth control, but it shouldn't be the right time."

"I'm clean, I promise. The Navy tests us all the time. And I've never gone bare with anyone before."

Brianna nodded as he ducked down and kissed her. He grabbed her red string bikini, the skimpy material looking even tinier in his firm grasp.

"Did I tell you how much I love you in this?" he asked huskily.

Brianna smiled. "Not in so many words. But I kind of gathered that when you ripped it right off me." She took his hand as he helped her sit up, and Matthew grinned as her breasts bounced. He lightly caressed the side of one, and then ran his fingertip around the areola. Her nipple instantly peaked again at his touch, and she couldn't believe she already felt aroused again.

"You're so gorgeous," he said in a low voice. "I hate that I'm leaving tonight."

Brianna reluctantly took her bikini top from him and tied it back on, much to Matthew's fascination. She tied the straps on the bottom as Matthew pulled his swim trunks back up and grabbed their towels.

"Come with me," he suddenly said.

"Where?"

"Back to Virginia Beach. I have to go back, you need a new job. It's perfect timing."

Brianna gave him a sad smile. "Perfect timing except Beckett will be back soon—hopefully—and my parents could use the help. Plus I can't just up and leave everything here. I don't have a job at the moment, but I'm waiting to hear back from a bunch of marketing firms."

"Just think about it," Matthew said, taking her hand. "It doesn't have to be today. But promise you'll consider it."

Brianna nodded as the thought took root in her mind. She could go visit him. Stay with him for a little while. But certainly he couldn't mean forever. And she couldn't ask him to make promises he couldn't keep.

# Chapter 14

"So he just left?" Ella asked the next afternoon. Brianna watched her add cream and sugar to her coffee as the two women sat in a sidewalk café down by the beach. A breeze blew in off the water, rustling the loose napkins on the table.

Brianna sipped her iced coffee, nodding. "Yeah. He had to go back for training this morning. Evan and Brent flew out with him last night."

"But you slept together. Twice!"

Brianna blushed, looking around. Although she didn't mind sharing some of the details with Ella, she didn't need the whole place listening in. Or all the random people walking by. She brushed her blonde hair back, glancing down at the pale pink top and white skinny jeans she had on. She felt pretty and pulled together today, and Matthew wasn't even around to see her. When he'd run into her having coffee over the weekend, she'd been in yoga pants and loose sweatshirt. "Technically, more than twice. He spent the entire night, and then there was the beach."

"Wow," Ella said, flashing her a huge smile. "I'm kind of shocked after the night you had at the bar. I'd be curled up in a ball and a complete wreck."

"Yeah, it just sort of happened. I mean, don't get me wrong, I've had a crush on him forever. My entire life. I'm not even sure he realized that. But he's one of those guys that never settle down, so I don't see anything happening. It was just the timing and stress of the situation."

"Well some of them settle down. What about Evan and his girlfriend? They live together and are having a baby."

Brianna paled slightly, thinking of the unprotected sex she'd had on the beach yesterday. She couldn't imagine Matthew ever wanting kids—not after what he'd told her the first night he'd been back in town. That a family didn't go with the life of a SEAL. And although she did want children, someday, now certainly wasn't the time. She'd be married with a house and job when that day came. Far off in the future.

"Are you okay?" Ella asked, looking concerned.

"Fine. Just thinking."

"And he did ask you to go back to Virginia Beach with him. I mean, guys don't just invite anyone to do that."

"Yeah, I know. But it was sort of in the heat of the moment. We'd just made love on the beach for heaven's sakes. Not even two nights ago he told me he'd never have a family. So my moving there to be with him for a while doesn't exactly add up to forever."

"Well, I find it hard to believe that he regularly asks women to come home with him. And what did he mean anyway by asking you to come with him—like move in together?"

Brianna shrugged, fiddling with the straw in her drink. "I have no idea. That's sort of the problem. We haven't discussed specifics about anything. We've known each other forever, but even so, you don't just abandon your own life for a guy like that."

"You do if he's that hot," Ella laughed.

Brianna raised her eyebrows.

"No, don't worry; I don't have a thing for Matthew. I just mean, those Navy SEALs were pretty easy on the eyes. Not to mention a hell of a lot nicer than most of the other men that I meet."

"You'll meet someone," Brianna assured her. "Not moonlighting as a cocktail waitress, but at school or somewhere you're supposed to be."

"Maybe, maybe not. But speaking of the bar, Frank left me two more messages."

"What?" Brianna asked, nearly dropping her iced coffee. "What did he say? I can't believe he'd call you again."

"First he asked me to come back, and then he said he'd withhold my paycheck unless I did."

"He can't do that," Brianna insisted. "You worked those hours, fair and square. Even if you up and quit without a good reason—which you did not—he has to pay you for the time you've already put in. He can't just make up his own rules."

"I know, but what am I supposed to do? I need the money for my tuition."

"Get another job. Any other job." Brianna looked

around the outdoor cafe they were currently relaxing in. "Work here if you have to. It's safe. It's money. I bet you could make some decent tips."

Ella laughed. "Look, we both know the reason you and I were there serving cocktails to a mostly male clientele—it paid well. Nearly twice as much as anywhere else I could work. I don't have a degree, remember? It's not like I have a lot of options."

"I know, I know. But promise me you won't go back there. I mean, I'd loan you the money if I had any. God, did I tell you Matthew wanted to pay my student loans? There's no way in hell I'd ever let him do that. He probably thinks I'm a complete idiot what with losing my job and then serving drinks. Some good my MBA did, huh?"

Ella shrugged. "Lots of people have to work their way through school. Look at me, look at everyone here," she said, gesturing around to the young waiters and waitresses. "And it's sort of sweet that he offered to pay them for you. I know you'd never accept money from him like that, but it must be nice to have someone care about you that much."

Brianna nodded, thoughtful. Of course Matthew cared about her—they'd practically grown up together. But caring about her didn't necessarily mean they had any sort of a future. It didn't mean that he wanted her to come to Virginia Beach forever.

"So anyway," Ella said. "What was the deal with your brother? You said you didn't want to talk about it yesterday over the phone, which I understand. Is he okay?"

Brianna frowned. "Yes and no. He's okay and stable right now, but the reason he didn't come home was because he tried to commit suicide on Saturday."

"Oh my God!" Ella said, covering her mouth with one hand. "I'm so sorry. I can't imagine what it must have been like hearing that after everything that happened at the bar. When did you find out?"

"My parents flew up there Saturday night before I got home. They left in such a rush they left me a note on the kitchen table."

"A note? That's horrible! They should've told you in person. Or waited until you got home."

"Yeah, probably so," Brianna said, blowing out a sigh. "They were in shock though. They've been through so much—first with fearing the worst after his accident, then dealing with his recovery and life as an amputee. We've all been looking forward to his coming home, and this was pretty much the last thing we ever expected. I thought he'd be happy to be alive. Not everyone makes it back."

"Are you going up there?" Ella asked. "To Walter Reed?"

"Next weekend. My parents are up there now and said to wait. They didn't want to overwhelm Beckett with visitors, and I think it'll be good to space out our visits. Hopefully it'll give him something to look forward to. It sucks though. I don't know what his state of mind is or anything. I want to just knock some sense into him, tell him he's lucky to be alive, but I know that's not how it works. It could be an even longer road to recovery after this."

"He's lucky to have you," Ella said. "I don't have any siblings, any parents. I know this is a tough time, but your family will be there for him. He's already got an advantage by having so many people care about him."

"You're right. It was just such a shock. I mean

when I talked to him Friday he sounded fine. I never expected him to do anything like this. Thank God he's okay. And hopefully when I get to see him, I can find out more."

Ella glanced at the time on her phone as the two women finished their drinks. "I hate to up and run, but I've got another paper to write."

"Yeah, I'll let you go. Thanks for meeting me for coffee."

Brianna tossed her empty cup in the garbage can as the two said goodbye. She sidestepped around a young couple making out on the sidewalk, rolling her eyes, and walked back to her car. She decided to quick check her email before she drove off to see if any prospective employers had emailed her. There was a note from her mother assuring her Beckett was doing okay and that they'd be back home in a day or so. She scrolled down some more and was surprised to see a quick note from Matthew.

> *Bri,*
> *Send me your resume. I may have a job lead for you.*
> *Matthew*

She looked quizzically at the email as if somehow more answers would materialize from the brief message. Matthew was in the Navy for God's sake. What kind of job could he possibly know about that she would be interested in? There was no mention of their weekend together or anything else, but he was at work, she reasoned. It's not like he'd be sending her a love letter or something. She smirked at the thought. He might kiss her until she was breathless and give her more orgasms that she could count, but Matthew wasn't exactly a romantic at heart.

Her mind flashed back to saying goodbye to him yesterday.

After making love on the beach, they'd picked up her car at the bar and driven home separately. Matthew had followed her inside, kissing and caressing her as they'd showered together. But there'd been no time for more lazy lovemaking in her bed. They'd said goodbye, and he'd disappeared back next door to pack and have his parents drop him off on base.

He'd promised to call tonight, but in the few hours they'd been apart, it was almost as if she could already feel him slipping away.

# Chapter 15

"I'm sorry to hear about your buddy," Patrick "Ice" Foster said to Matthew as they changed in the locker room. Their SEAL team had done grueling dives out in the choppy water, and Matthew's muscles were already feeling fatigued.

Hell.

He'd love to take another long, hot shower with Brianna right now, watching the water spill down over her gorgeous curves. Kissing her breasts and teasing her soft folds with his tongue. It was hard to believe that was only twenty-four hours ago; it felt like a damn near lifetime.

"It sucks," Matthew muttered, slamming his locker shut. He glanced over at his team leader, who was appraising him with cool blue eyes. "Not every man's lucky enough to make it home, you know, Ice? And for a guy to try to take his own life? It just doesn't make sense. Beckett was like a brother to me. I'm the one who got him to join the Navy all those years ago. I already felt guilty as hell about him getting injured and losing a limb. Now he tries to off himself and what do I do? Spend the night with his sister."

Patrick raised his eyebrows.

"Yeah, didn't I mention that? The woman I was with all weekend is my neighbor and my buddy's kid sister. She's 26 now—"

"Not exactly a kid then," Patrick pointed out.

"Hell no. She's all woman. But a man doesn't go after his friend's sister. It's like guy code or something."

Patrick nodded, smirking. "Maybe not, but it didn't sound to me like you were chasing after her. You protected her—saved her from some jackass in a place she probably never should have been working. And what happened after in the heat of the moment? Well, it takes two to tango."

"Hell yeah," Brent hooted as he walked in to the locker room. "And that woman was fine, I'll tell you that. I'd tango with her any day if she wasn't already Gator's."

Matthew coughed, nearly choking. Was she his? The men on his SEAL team seemed to think so. Too bad convincing his best friend might be another story.

"Who's this?" Christopher "Blade" Walters asked as he walked in behind Brent. He dropped his gear onto the ground, opening up his locker.

"No one," Matthew ground out at the exact same time that Brent said, "Gator's woman."

"The hell if I know what's going on," Patrick grumbled. "Thank God I found Rebecca, because some days I have a hard time keeping up with the rest of you."

Brent guffawed, and Matthew shook his head in disbelief. "Speaking of Rebecca, thanks for that tip on the job lead in her office," Matthew said.

"What job?" Christopher asked.

"A marketing position for her law firm. They're looking to bring in new clientele and expand. I think they worked with marketing agencies in the past but are considering bringing someone on board full time. Brianna might be interested."

"The woman who's a cocktail waitress?" Christopher asked, puzzled.

Matthew's gaze slid to Brent, his eyes steel. What the hell had Brent been telling everyone? "That was just a temporary job," Matthew said coolly. "She's an MBA and former marketing exec."

"Gotcha," Christopher said. "If she's smart like Lexi, you better watch out," he joked.

Matthew laughed, thinking of Christopher's computer hacker fiancée. Christopher was a computer whiz in his own right, but Lexi was his match in every way. Those two also had a past—they'd been together ten years ago out in Coronado and broken up before recently making a go of things. Somehow they'd worked out their differences and were now engaged. Could he do the same with Brianna? Sure, she'd always been the girl next door, but things had shifted between them this weekend. And it was no small change—more like a seismic shift in the way he saw the whole damn world.

Life was funny sometimes.

Not even two days after he first told Brianna that he'd never have a family, he was starting to wish for a life like that with her.

Imagine that.

He grabbed his gear, saying goodbye to the other men as he headed out for the night. He needed food and needed to unpack from the weekend away, but first, he needed to call Brianna.

*\*\*\**

The phone rang as she sat on her bed, laptop propped in her lap, responding to emails. She'd gotten two bites on the resumes she'd sent out last week. Neither were exactly her dream job—one was a step down from her last position but local. The other was in Northern Florida, which meant she'd have to leave her family. The whole idea sticking it out in the bar had been to wait until the perfect local job showed up.

But what if that never happened?

She reached over to her nightstand and saw Matthew's name flash across the screen of her cell.

"Hi," she said softly as she answered. She set her laptop to the side and stretched out on her bed, clad only in a soft tank top and floral sleep shorts. Oddly enough, Matthew had never actually called her before. Growing up together, he'd just shown up at their front door. And as they grew older, he was always more of Beckett's friend than hers. It felt oddly intimate to be sitting here on her bed with Matthew's voice at her ear. The exact same bed in which she'd spent the night in his arms.

"Hi, darlin'," he drawled, and she giggled.

"How was training?"

"Brutal. My entire body aches, and I wish I was there with you."

"So I could kiss all the boo-boos away?" she

teased.

"Something like that," he murmured, his voice growing husky.

"I heard back from two potential employers," she said, changing the subject. The thought of kissing Matthew was too much to bear right now. She wanted him here, too, and they'd barely been apart one day.

"Really? That's great. Did you get my email earlier? Patrick's girlfriend Rebecca is a lawyer at a firm here in Virginia Beach. They're looking to expand and hire a marketing consultant. It sounded like something you might be interested in. Plus then you'd be here with me."

"Yeah, that does sound like it could have potential."

"So are you going to send me your resume? I'll forward it on to her if you want."

"Uh, sure."

There was a pause before Matthew cleared his throat and spoke. "Look, Bri—I didn't expect anything to happen this weekend when I was home. Hell, I didn't exactly expect anything to happen between us ever. But now that it finally has? I want to keep seeing you."

"Yeah, me too. But I'm just not even sure how that would work with my living in Florida and you up in Virginia. We'd basically be starting out in a long-distance relationship."

"That makes the job at Rebecca's law firm sound pretty damn good. It's right here in Virginia Beach; we could be together."

"Well, what would I do? Get my own apartment there?"

"If you wanted. Although I'd love to have you

living with me—spending every night in my bed, waking up each morning in my arms."

"Doesn't it seem too sudden?"

Matthew chuckled. "Maybe. But I've known you my entire life. Your entire life, at least," he corrected. She could practically see him grinning on the other end of the phone. "All I know is that I want you with me. When I saw that guy grabbing you in the hallway—hell, Bri. It just about damn near ripped my heart out. It opened my eyes though. I want you here with me."

"I'll send you the resume," she promised. "I mean, if the job doesn't work out, then there's no point in even trying to figure out the rest—the living arrangements and what not. There's just a lot going on at the moment, and I need to figure out what's best. I have to take whatever marketing position I can find."

"If you did come here, move here I mean, I'll have to tell Beckett. He has a right to know. I need to go see him anyway."

"I was going to fly up there next weekend."

"When are your parents coming home?"

"Tomorrow. He's doing good, I suppose, according to my mom. I mean considering the circumstances. But I'm planning to go there on Friday. Hopefully with some treatment for PTSD he can come home and then continue seeing a doctor down here."

"They should have someone on base," Matthew said. "I can help if you need me to."

"That'd be great. I don't even have the first clue where to start."

"Would it be okay if I crash on your visit with

Beckett next weekend? I'd probably drive up late Friday. But then I'd get to see both of you. Maryland is a helluva lot closer than Florida."

"That sounds good," Brianna said. "But what should we tell him about us? He's already stressed enough."

"I'll talk to him," Matthew assured her. "I think it needs to be between us guys."

"If you're sure."

"Absolutely. And I can't wait to see you."

"Me either. I already made hotel arrangements for the weekend. Do you, uh, want to stay with me?"

"Hell yeah," Matthew said. "There's nothing I want more, sweetheart." He yawned a moment later, and Brianna giggled.

"Am I that boring to talk to?" she teased.

"Training was brutal, darlin'. And I didn't exactly get a ton of sleep over the weekend. Not that I minded that one bit."

"So I'll talk to you sometime this week? I can email you the hotel info."

"Absolutely. I wish I was there to kiss you goodnight. Hell, who am I kidding? I wish I could do a lot more than just kiss you."

"Me too," she admitted.

"The weekend can't get here soon enough then. Goodnight, Bri."

"Goodnight," she said as she disconnected the call.

A weekend with Matthew. It almost felt like they were making it official by telling her brother. That still didn't solve the long distance issue, her lack of a job, or anything else. But the idea of seeing Matthew again soothed her, somehow, and she yawned. Glancing at her clock, she saw it was only nine p.m. But after her crazy weekend, she needed to catch up on her rest. She'd worry about everything else tomorrow.

# Chapter 16

Brianna cursed at the winds whipping outside the kitchen window on Friday morning. The trees swayed dangerously close to the ground, debris flew through the air, and rain battered the sides and roof of the house. The tropical storm blowing through town meant all flights were cancelled for the day, possibly for the entire weekend. So much for flying up to see Beckett tonight or getting to see Matthew again.

She sank into a chair at the kitchen table, casting one last look out the window. The angry storm clouds matched her current mood. She took a sip of her steaming hot coffee and flipped open her laptop, scrolling through her emails.

She'd set up an interview for next week with the local company she'd sent a resume to, but to her surprise, the job lead Matthew had told her about had resulted in a hit as well. The woman, Rebecca, who was dating a member of Matthew's SEAL team had called her yesterday. They'd chatted a bit and Brianna had done a brief phone screening with their HR department. She had an interview lined up in Virginia Beach in two weeks for the new marketing position at the law firm.

She hardly dared to hope the job would come through, but a week after Matthew had gone back, she was itching to see him again. It didn't help that she was currently unemployed. She might not have exactly enjoyed working as a cocktail waitress, but at least it gave her something to do. With her parents gone for several days, she'd mostly been at the house, culling through the classifieds and sending out resume after resume.

"That's nice of your office to let you work from home today," her mom commented as she walked into the kitchen.

Brianna cringed. She still hadn't fessed up that she'd actually been laid off. Her parents had been so shaken when they'd returned from Walter Reed earlier in the week, though, that she didn't have the heart to confess she was currently unemployed. And had been for a while.

"Nothing's open today," Brianna casually said. "Including the airport."

"Have you talked to your brother?"

"Yeah, he was disappointed I can't come but is looking forward to my visit next weekend instead. His spirits seemed up."

"I worry that's just the medication they have him on. He's taking antidepressants."

"Oh. Right."

"We saw a change just in the few days we were there. But once they lower his dosage, there's always the possibility of him becoming depressed again. He'll be meeting with counselors, but he was before, and look what happened."

"Maybe if we check in with him more," Brianna said thoughtfully. "Matthew said he'd get up there to see him also."

"I just wish Beckett was back home," her mom said worriedly. "Then we could keep an eye on him."

"He'll be here soon enough," Brianna assured her.

Her phone buzzed on the kitchen table, and she grabbed it, seeing Matthew's name on the screen. Her mother excused herself as Brianna answered.

"Hi darlin'," he said. "I just caught the weather on CNN. It looks like flying up tonight is a no-go with the tropical storm."

"Yeah, it's bad out. I'm sure we'll lose power before long."

"It's not supposed to hit our area for another day or so. I may still go up tonight to see Beckett. It's easy enough for me to make the drive, and I don't want both of us to be no-shows."

"He'd like that," Brianna said. "But are you going to talk to him?"

"About us?"

"Yeah. I just thought I'd be there when you did. I know he's injured and all, but he's my older brother. I might have to pull him off of you," she joked.

"You don't think I could take Beckett?" Matthew teased. "That was harsh."

Brianna laughed. "I worry what you two could do to each other if given the chance."

"Actually, I was thinking of heading up two weekends in a row. I'll just drive up this evening for one night to see him like we planned, and then next weekend I'll drive up again when you're there. We could talk with him then."

"And your CO will let you do that? Take two weekends in a row?"

"Given the circumstances, he's pretty understanding. And although being several hours away isn't ideal, I can haul ass back if need be. We're on call 24/7, but I arranged to be off next weekend when I'm up there with you."

"I'd love to see you then. I was pretty disappointed the tropical storm came through this weekend. Talk about awful timing."

"Me too," he said, his voice gruff. "I was looking forward to it more than you know."

The lights flickered, and Brianna glanced around the kitchen. "It looks like we're about to lose power. Hopefully my cell connection will hold."

"All right, I'll let you go. I'm on my way to PT anyway. Tell my parents I checked in if you see them. I'll call you when I get up to Walter Reed tonight. Stay safe in the storm."

"I will. Talk you soon."

They disconnected, and Brianna gaze again fell to the rain outside, her mind wandering. She wondered what a day in Matthew's life would be like—always training to stay in top physical shape, drilling for missions. It was so different than everything she did. All that she knew. Plus a lot of it involved dangerous operations—things she could never know about. Look at her own brother—he'd barely survived his latest deployment. Could she live knowing Matthew would always in that type of danger as well?

She restlessly glanced back at her laptop. She'd have battery life to continue working if the power failed but couldn't exactly continue sending out emails to prospective employers with Internet access. Her mind wasn't in it anyway right now. It looked like it would be the perfect day to curl up with a good book and forget everything else.

\*\*\*

Matthew tucked his cell back into his shorts pocket as he walked down the hall to the weight room. He'd talked to Bri every night this week, and that quick call wasn't nearly long enough. He loved the sweet sound of her voice, the tiny gasps and giggles she made over the phone. He could almost picture the expression on her face most of the time. Would almost pretend that she was right there beside him.

When the hell had he become the kind of man who liked to sit around chatting on his cell every night? With Brianna he could easily talk for hours, wanting to learn every last thing about her. He knew her childhood as well as he knew his own, but to learn about the woman she'd become during their time apart? He'd gladly spend a lifetime finding out all the tiny details. But they had PT this morning and then drills all afternoon. He didn't have time to sit down for a long talk. He worried about Brianna, her parents, and his own weathering the tropical storm. It wasn't the first they'd seen in Pensacola and sure the hell wouldn't be the last, but he couldn't help feeling regret that he wasn't there. And wasn't that the crux of his whole problem. Even if Bri moved here to Little Creek, he'd be gone a hell of a lot.

Could she handle that?

Could he?

Still, it would be pretty fucking spectacular to wake up beside her each day. There was a possessive, alpha male instinct in him that wanted Bri in his bed. Hell, her floral scent on his sheets would make him as hard as a rock. Add in all that long blonde hair combined with her supple curves, and he'd be lucky if he ever made it out of bed. He'd be willing to sacrifice a good night's sleep for night after night with her.

And to take care of her, protect her, and have a woman to come home to? He thought he'd never want something like that, but with Bri, it seemed almost inevitable.

He grinned as he walked into the weight room, and Evan raised his eyebrows. "Someone's in a good mood today."

"Just hoping the whole job situation with Brianna will work out so that she can move up here."

"Move as in move in with you?"

"Hell, that's what I'm hoping. It's up to her though. I know she doesn't want to rush into things, but I've known her for a lifetime."

"Have you guys told Beckett yet?"

"Nope," Matthew laughed. "He might just kill me when he finds out."

"So I should look for your body tomorrow morning?" Evan asked.

"Negative. That tropical storm just messed up my weekend plans. Bri can't fly out, so she's postponing her trip until next weekend."

"You still heading up to see Beckett?"

"That's the plan. Just for the night though."

Evan laughed. "So what makes you think he won't wring your neck? That seems even more likely without Brianna there to soften the blow."

Matthew chuckled. "She had that same thought. We're planning to tell him next weekend when we're both there. Her call. Personally I'd like to just let him know now. That guy is like a brother to me, but I have to respect her wishes."

"Any more word on that asshole in jail?" Evan asked, grabbing some of the free weights as he began his set of reps.

"Still rotting in his jail cell. And he will be until the trail unless he strikes a plea bargain. Either way he'll be doing jail time, which makes me feel a helluva lot better. I still wouldn't mind smashing his face in though."

The rest of the team walked into the weight room, and Matthew headed over to one of the machines, ready to start lifting.

"Whose face are you going to smash in?" Brent asked, curiosity sparking in his eyes as he sauntered over.

"That asshole that attacked Bri. He's in jail though, so I guess I missed my chance."

"That's right where he fucking belongs," Brent muttered.

"Yep. I couldn't agree with you more."

The other men spread out amongst the weights and equipment, and Matthew let his thoughts drift back to Brianna as he worked on his quads. Hell, another week apart felt like a damn eternity. He'd been looking forward to seeing her for days. How did men deploy for months, an entire year, without seeing their families? Somehow they made it work. And if he somehow got the stars to align in his favor, so would he.

# Chapter 17

Brianna hopped into a shuttle at National Airport the following Friday night, catching a ride to her hotel near Walter Reed. After putting her visit off for a week, she was excited and anxious to see both Matthew and Beckett. Although they'd talked most nights, her heart pounded at the idea of seeing Matthew again this evening. How was she supposed to act around him when they visited her brother? Beckett would see right through her the minute they walked in the room. Maybe she should let Matthew talk to him first, like he'd wanted. She'd wait outside while they discussed things man-to-man, and then they could all have their happy reunion.

If only it was guaranteed to go as smoothly as she wanted.

She looked out the window of the shuttle, taking in the bumper-to-bumper traffic. It seemed like every time she was up in the DC area, traffic was brutal, and this Friday night was no exception. Matthew had offered to drive to the airport to pick her up, but since Bethesda was on the other side of the Beltway, up in Maryland, she'd opted to use airport transportation. It saved Matthew some travel time with the horrible Friday night traffic and would give them all longer to visit tonight.

She sent off a quick text to them both, letting them know her plane had landed and she was on her way to Bethesda. Nearly two hours later, after crawling along in bumper-to-bumper traffic, she finally stepped off the shuttle at her hotel. She felt a sudden wave of dizziness as she lugged her suitcase down the bus steps, and she clutched onto the metal railing, trying to regain her balance. The driver hastily moved to assist her, asking if she was all right, but she brushed it off, realizing that she hadn't eaten a single thing since lunch.

Her phone buzzed with a text from Matthew:
*Great. Can't wait to see you, sweetheart.*

She did a quick double-take and realized he'd only texted her back, not Beckett. A bellhop walked over to collect her suitcase, and she swayed slightly as she looked up at him.

"Are you all right, miss?" the older gentleman asked.

"Uh, yeah, I'm fine. It's just been a long day," she assured him.

"Visiting someone at the medical center?"

"My brother. I was supposed to come in last week but my flight was cancelled because of a tropical storm down in Florida."

He nodded, and she followed him into the lobby, deciding to go ahead and check into her room.

Hopefully Matthew would be getting in soon, but he could call her when he arrived. There was no point in sitting around waiting for him. After getting her keycard from the clerk at the front desk, she took the elevator up to the eighth floor. She wheeled her suitcase down the long hallway and finally made it to her room, feeling completely exhausted. After her long day of travel, she decided to quick shower and change before meeting the guys. Hopefully Matthew would arrive by the time she finished getting ready, and they could go see her brother together.

She pulled fresh clothes from her suitcase and unpacked her toiletries, then carried them into the bathroom. She pulled out her floral shampoo and favorite soap, but her heart stopped as her gaze fell on the unopened box of tampons she'd packed.

She was never, ever late, but her period was due two days ago, and she didn't have so much as a single sign of it. Uneasiness washed over her as she recalled her day on the beach with Matthew. More specifically, her memory of them making love behind the dunes without using a condom.

It was impossible, she reasoned. It would have been past the middle of the month when they'd had sex, and even so, it was way too early to be feeling any sort of pregnancy symptoms. Didn't women not feel those until they were several months along? Morning sickness and all that? Most likely her period was late from the stress of traveling and seeing her brother.

A little voice in the back of her head reminded her that missing her period was in fact a pregnancy symptom, but she tried to ignore the sudden feelings of panic.

She turned on the water in the shower, stepping

THE SEAL NEXT DOOR

inside when it was finally warm enough. The hot water washed over her, easing the tension in her muscles. She twisted under the spray, trying to avoid getting her hair wet, and felt a strange little pull in her abdomen. It didn't hurt but just felt…different. It had to be her imagination though. Even if she was somehow pregnant—which she was not—there was no way she'd notice any changes so soon.

Right?

She quickly finished rinsing off, then turned off the water and grabbed a fluffy, white towel. Wrapping it around herself without bothering to completely towel off, she walked into the room and pulled her phone from her purse. Opening up the calendar app, she recalculated the numbers again.

Shakily, she speed-dialed Ella.

"Hey, did you make it up to Bethesda safely? How's your brother?"

"I think I'm pregnant," Brianna blurted out. Drops of water ran down her legs onto the carpet, but she ignored them and sank dripping wet onto the bed, tears filling her eyes.

"What? Are you serious?"

"Yeah, I'm serious. I'm late. I'm *never* late."

"Is Matthew there?"

"God, no. I haven't even seen him yet. But when we were on the beach his last day in Pensacola, we didn't use any protection. I know it was stupid, but it was sort of the heat of the moment."

"Did you take a pregnancy test? You've been under a lot of stress lately. I'm always irregular, so I'm not the best person to get advice from, but it's totally possible the stress just messed up your cycle this month. There has been a lot going on."

"I know, you're right. There's been too much going on. I just feel like something's different—I can't even explain it. I was lightheaded earlier, and I can just tell that something isn't right. I feel different."

"Are you near a drug store? Go buy a pregnancy test. Before you see Matthew, otherwise he'll wonder what's wrong. Take the test just to put your mind at ease. It's probably nothing, but there's no sense worrying about it."

"You're right; I'm sure it's nothing," Brianna said as she shakily stood back up. "It was just that one time, and like you said, stress can mess with your body."

"Exactly. Go buy it, take the test, and call me back. And after that's all taken care of, go see your brother and spend the night with your man."

Brianna laughed weakly.

"Come on, you've been looking forward to seeing Matthew all week. Take care of this, and everything will be fine. But don't forget to call me the second you find out."

"Okay, bye," Brianna whispered.

She dropped her phone onto the bed as she stood, and it instantly buzzed with an incoming text.

*Should be there in 30. See you soon, darlin'.*

Brianna burst into tears. Suddenly thirty minutes felt way too soon.

\*\*\*

Shakily, Brianna sank onto the bed in her hotel room twenty minutes later. She'd thrown on jeans and a tee shirt, not even bothering to reapply make-up, and her blonde hair was pulled up in a messy twist. She looked like a wreck and she knew it, but something in her gut convinced her she was right. She glanced at the timer on her phone, seeing that only thirty seconds had passed. The pregnancy test she'd bought said it needed three minutes, and she'd left it in the bathroom as she waited, unable to watch.

Her heart pounded in her chest and her palms began sweating. Matthew was going to be here any minute and would know something was wrong the second he looked at her. Hastily, she sent him a quick text:

*Change of plans. Meet me in Beckett's room.*

She took a deep breath and got a message back from Matthew simply saying okay. That was one problem down. She'd put off seeing him for the moment at least.

Three minutes had to have passed by now, right?

She stood, and steeling herself, walked into the bathroom. The pregnancy test lay innocently on the counter where she'd left it, but her heart stopped as she saw the two pink lines.

She was pregnant.

# Chapter 18

Matthew parked his pick-up in the parking lot at Walter Reed and climbed out of the driver seat, stretching his sore muscles. The drive up had taken nearly six hours, which was insane, but what did he expect with Friday night traffic. He was puzzled that Bri wanted to meet here instead of her hotel, but maybe she'd been anxious to see her brother, he reasoned. He would've loved a little private time before they came over to give her a kiss hello and pull her into his arms, but he couldn't fault her for wanting to spend some extra time with Beckett rather than waiting around for him to arrive.

He walked in, flashing his military ID, and made his way through the same hallways he'd come down last weekend. Hell. It would be good to see his buddy and great to see Brianna. Had she already told Beckett about them, he wondered?

The door to Beckett's room was open, so Matthew walked in, his eyes sweeping the small space and not noticing Brianna or any of her things. Beckett was resting on the hospital bed, covered in a thin white blanket. His dark hair was cropped short, and he'd shaved. Faint red lines traced down his neck from where shrapnel had hit, and a long scar ran down his left arm. But all in all, he looked good.

"Hey buddy," Beckett called out as he walked in. "About time you got your ass in here."

Matthew chuckled and walked over, fist-bumping his friend, before sitting down in the chair near his bedside. "Traffic up here is brutal. You're lucky I came at all."

"I know, I know. You just couldn't resist my charm."

"Where's Bri?" Matthew asked. "I thought she was already here."

Beckett raised his eyebrows, the sea green eyes identical to his sister's sparking with curiosity. "Brianna isn't here yet. Why?"

Matthew swallowed, realizing his error. "She texted to say she was on her way over."

Beckett frowned. "What time?"

"Half an hour ago, maybe. I guess something held her up."

"So why's she texting you and not me?" Beckett asked, not missing a beat. "Something I'm missing here?"

Matthew blew out a sigh. "Look, your sister wanted to tell you when we were here together, but we're, uh, sort of seeing each other."

Beckett started laughing, and Matthew released a breath he hadn't realized that he'd been holding.

"Well, it's about damn time. She's only been in love with you forever."

Matthew's chest clenched as he nailed his friend with a gaze. "Well why the fuck didn't you ever say anything?"

"Hell, she was too young when we left. Not even in high school yet. She had to grow up, and you always had a trail of girls chasing after you. Maybe we all had to grow up a bit first."

Matthew leaned back in the chair, crossing his legs. "You're probably right, but damn. I was always asking your mom about her when I was back in town. I'm just kind of amazed we never got together sooner."

Beckett shrugged, wincing at the movement. "You were too dumb to see it, I guess."

"You're lucky you're in a hospital bed," Matthew threatened.

"So what's going to happen now? You're in Little Creek; she's down in Pensacola. Did she find a new marketing job?"

"She told you about that?"

"Well, I knew she got laid off and was working as a cocktail waitress for a while. I told her to quit that months ago."

Matthew shifted uneasily, and Beckett suddenly struggled to sit up, his heart rate increasing on the monitor. "Shit, is she still working there?"

"No, she's not," Matthew assured him, watching the monitor closely. Hell. This wasn't exactly the time to tell Beckett about the incident at the bar. Maybe when he recovered and was home in Florida.

They heard a rustling in the hallway, and Matthew glanced up, expecting Brianna to walk in. No one entered the room, though, so he figured it was just someone passing by.

"So what's gonna happen then? Do the long distance thing?" Beckett asked as he relaxed again.

"I'm trying to convince her to move up to Virginia Beach."

"And move in with you?"

Matthew grinned. "That's the plan, but it's up to your sister."

"And then what, marriage, kids?"

"Whoa, hold up," Matthew said chuckling. "No one said anything about that. Let's take it one step at a time."

At that moment, Brianna came rushing into the room, looking pale with tears in her eyes. Matthew jumped to his feet, and Beckett asked if she was okay. She looked between both of them and shook her head. "I'm sorry, I have to go. I shouldn't be here." She turned and fled from the room as quickly as she'd come.

Matthew and Beckett exchanged a glance.

"Well don't sit around waiting for me," Beckett chastised. "I've got one leg. Go after her!"

Matthew bolted from the room, looking left and right to see where she'd run off to. His heart clenched at the tears in her eyes and the frail way she'd looked. Something was wrong, and he had to find her. Immediately. He raced down toward the elevator bank, looking around, but Brianna was already gone.

\*\*\*

Brianna rushed out the doors of Walter Reed, ignoring the stares of curious onlookers. Tears streamed down her cheeks, and she gasped for breath.

When she'd first heard the guys talking, she thought Matthew was going to tell Beckett about the incident in the bar, and she'd hesitated outside the door to her brother's room. But the conversation after that was a million times worse. Matthew had just about said outright that he didn't want kids.

And she was pregnant.

With his baby.

Sobs came from her chest as she rushed down the sidewalk into a secluded courtyard.

It was bad enough having the shock of an unplanned pregnancy, but to have to deal with it alone? It was overwhelming.

She sank onto a bench near a fountain and let the tears come. She needed to get out of here as quickly as possible, but she'd have to arrange for another flight. The idea of sitting in traffic again on that damn shuttle bus back to the airport and then waiting around the airport made the trip feel impossible to make at the moment. She needed to rest, to cry herself to sleep, and then just deal with everything else in the morning.

Her phone buzzed from inside her purse, and she knew it was Matthew, but she ignored it.

*He didn't want kids.*

Fresh tears streamed down her cheeks, and she felt a wave of nausea wash over her. What was she supposed to do now?

She wiped the tears from her face with her hands, knowing she was being ridiculous. She hadn't even said hello to her own brother, but she couldn't face going back there right now. She'd have to check into a new hotel, she decided. Matthew knew where she was staying because they were supposed to be together.

*Together.*

Her body shook as she wrapped her arms around herself. It was hard to imagine feeling more alone than she did at the moment. But she wasn't alone. She had life, a baby, growing inside her.

"Bri!"

Matthew's deep voice washed over her like a caress, and for a moment she wondered how he'd found her. She longed to run to him, to sob into his chest, to make him promise it would all be okay. But he was the one who'd inadvertently made her so upset in the first place. She was shocked at the positive test results but it was his words that had sent her into a tailspin.

He rushed over and knelt down in front of her, taking one of her hands in his. "What happened? Are you okay?" He wiped away her tears with his other hand, and she clung to him like he was her lifeline in the midst of the storm. Concerned green eyes met hers, and he actually looked scared that something was really wrong.

"I'm pregnant," she blurted out.

Matthew did a double-take. "Wait. What?"

"I'm pregnant," she repeated. "I was late, and I just took the test. And I heard you talking to my brother. I heard you saying you don't want kids."

"Wait. Slow down. Are you sure?"

"Of course I'm sure!" she said, sobs escaping again.

"I'm sorry, I didn't mean—" He pulled her against his chest as he knelt before her, stroking her hair with one hand. "Shhh. Don't cry."

She sobbed into his shirt, feeling the solid strength

of him. Muscular arms wrapped around her, holding her close, keeping her safe. Matthew kissed the top of her head gently, murmuring into her ear. When the tears finally slowed, he held her, looking down into her eyes. "I can't believe we're going to have a baby," he whispered.

"You want a baby?"

"Hell, I want everything with you, Bri. I was surprised, that's all. But I already told you I want you to move in with me, to wake up in my arms each morning. To know my child is growing inside you? That's pretty amazing stuff. I couldn't ask for anything more."

She smiled at him through her tears, and he ducked down and kissed her gently.

"Can we go back to the hotel? We'll go see my brother tomorrow. I just need to let everything sink in first."

"Of course, sweetheart. Don't you know I'd do anything for you?"

She burst into tears again, and Matthew gently wiped them away. They walked to Matthew's pick-up truck and drove back to the hotel. When they got back to the room, Brianna caught sight of herself in the mirror and cringed. "I look terrible."

"You look perfect," he said, coming up behind her. He wrapped his arms around her, pulling her close. One held her securely across her chest, while he let his other hand rest on her still flat stomach. She felt his chest rising and falling behind her and his erection digging into her lower back. "You're perfect," he breathed again, kissing the top of her head. She tilted her head back, and he ducked to kiss her, claiming her mouth with his. One hand slid to her breast, cupping it through the material of her shirt, and she moaned softly.

"Can I make love to you?" he asked gently. "Do you feel okay?"

"Yes," she whispered.

His hand on her stomach slid to the waist of her jeans, and he unbuttoned them, slowly sliding down the zipper. She watched in the mirror in fascination as his large hand slid into her pants. It looked erotic and sexy-as-hell, not to mention possessive.

*His.*

*She was his.*

He cupped her sex for a moment, holding her to him, and then his fingers delved into her lace panties. His other hand slid under the v-neck of her shirt, beneath her bra, cupping her breast. She was still fully clothed but completely aroused, lost to his touch.

His fingers slid through her wetness, finding her clit, and he circled around slowly. She gasped as pleasure surged through her, and he worked his hand faster, driving her up, sending her spiraling out of control. She cried out his name as she came, her inner walls clamping down around nothing. She longed to have him filling her, taking her, claiming her.

"Hell, you're wet," he murmured. "So wet for me."

He tugged off her tee shirt, slowly unfastening her bra so that her breasts bounced free. Her gaze met Matthew's in the mirror, and his eyes were on fire. He cupped her breasts with large hands, massaging them gently as he ground his erection against her from behind. He lightly pinched both of her nipples, and she squealed in surprise.

"I'm really sensitive now," she said.

"Sorry, I'll be gentle," he promised. Matthew slid down her jeans and panties, helping her to step free of them, and quickly undressed himself. He pulled her body to his, his thick erection digging into her lower back. The sight of their naked bodies in the mirror seemed almost illicit. She'd never watched herself making love before, but somehow the idea of watching Matthew taking her, claiming her, made her even more desperate for him.

"I guess I don't need a condom?" he asked wryly.

Brianna let out a soft laugh. "Not anymore."

Matthew ducked and kissed the side of her neck. "I love the feel of going bare inside you. You feel so good around me, Bri." He gently spread her legs and bent her over the dresser, his large body curling around hers. One hand cupped a breast, and she felt his erection prodding between her legs as he guided himself to her entrance.

She met his eyes in the mirror, gasping as he lightly caressed her breast. "You are so fucking gorgeous," he murmured. "So beautiful."

He slid inside of her slowly, his thick length penetrating and stretching her. His hand clasped possessively on her hip, and he gently rocked into her, causing her to moan in pleasure.

"Matthew," she gasped. Her inner walls clamped down around him, and he was deep, so deep when he took her this way. He thrust gently, slowly, and she again caught sight of their bodies in the mirror. Matthew was all strength and muscles, curled protectively, possessively around her smaller frame. The way he held her was a claiming, a possession. But he was so gentle it nearly brought tears to her eyes.

He bucked into her more quickly, beginning to

lose some of his control, and his hand slid to where their sexes were joined. He stroked her clit lightly as he filled her, and she cried out, surrendering to the sensations, falling off the precipice as he made her come around his hardened cock. He stiffened and then spilled his seed inside her, grunting as he released.

Afterward he bent and lifted her, carrying her into the shower where he washed her hair and body. When they were both clean and dry, they slipped beneath the covers. Matthew's large frame covered hers, and he kissed and caressed her, worshipping her, letting her know this was exactly where he wanted to be.

# Epilogue

"How many clothes do you have anyway?" Matthew joked as he hauled yet another box of her clothing into his apartment in Virginia Beach. Evan and Brent walked in behind him, each carrying large boxes as well.

"Not nearly enough," Brianna joked from where she rested on the sofa, sipping decaf iced tea. Evan's girlfriend Ali and Ella sat beside her, laughing.

"She's right, Matthew," Ali said. "And she'll need even more clothes once she finally starts showing." Ali gestured to her own stomach, now round with Evan's child.

"I kind of dread buying maternity clothes," Brianna admitted. "Baby clothes are so much cuter."

"I'll take you shopping," Ali promised.

Matthew walked over on his way back out to the rental truck and ducked down to brush a kiss across Brianna's lips. "I should help you," she said. "I feel bad you guys are doing all the work."

"No way," Matthew said. "That's why I brought in reinforcements." He gestured to Evan and Brent as they walked out of the spare bedroom.

"Looks like you don't have a guest room anymore," Evan laughed. "Soon it will be filled up with baby gear."

Brianna smiled, her face flushing with happiness. "Honestly, I can't wait. Between the new job, finally moving in with Matthew, and expecting a little one? I'm so excited that I could just burst."

"You deserve it after the crazy few months you've had," Ella said with a grin. Brent's eyes slid to Ella, but he walked out without a word.

"Is he always in such a good mood?" Brianna asked, raising her eyebrows.

"Ignore him," Matthew and Evan said at the same time, and the women laughed.

After the truck had finally been unloaded and everyone else had left for the day, Matthew pulled Brianna into his arms. "It took a long time to get all the details nailed down, but hell, this was worth the wait. I love the idea of you living here with me. Of us—together as a family." A grin a mile wide spread across his face, and Brianna beamed up at him.

He trailed his fingers down her bare arm, sending shivers racing down her spine. One touch from Matthew was all it took to make her come undone. And now rather than being limited to seeing each other only on weekends, she was finally here.

Beckett had moved in with her parents after being released from Walter Reed, she'd gotten the job at the law firm and moved out, and life was as it should be. Ella was on her spring break from college and had tagged along to help her move in and get settled, and as Brianna had met the other women who were dating the men on Matthew's SEAL team, she'd made new friends as well.

"I can hardly believe it worked out this way," Brianna admitted. "Everything's perfect."

"I love you," Matthew said, his voice deep.

"I love you, too."

"Everything is pretty damn perfect. There's just one thing left that I need to do," Matthew said, a gleam in his eye.

Brianna gasped as Matthew fell to one knee, pulling a small velvet box from his pocket. He flipped it open, revealing a sparkling diamond engagement ring nestled inside. "I've known you my whole life, Brianna. Growing up, we were hardly ever apart. And although I was a fool to let so many years slip by, I don't want to spend another second without you in my life. I want us to share a life together. Have a family and grow old together. I love you so much, Bri. Will you marry me?"

"Yes," she whispered, tears of happiness filling her eyes. "Yes, of course!"

Matthew slipped the ring on her trembling hand, and then stood, ducking down to steal her breath in a searing kiss. She was finally his. Forever.

# About the Author

USA Today Bestselling Author Makenna Jameison writes sizzling romantic suspense, including the addictive Alpha SEALs series. Makenna loves the beach, strong coffee, red wine, and traveling. She lives in Washington DC with her husband and two daughters.

Visit www.makennajameison.com to discover your next great read.

# Want to read more from MAKENNA JAMEISON?

## Keep reading for an exclusive excerpt from the sixth book in her Alpha SEALs series, *PROTECTED BY A SEAL*.

Navy SEAL Brent "Cobra" Rollins never met a woman he didn't want. He's gotten more action than his entire SEAL team combined, but the gorgeous brunette he barely even touched is the one he can't get out of his head.

Ella Thompson is working her way through school, and the cocky, assertive Navy SEAL who stood up for her is also wrong in about a thousand different ways. Player? Check. Older man? Check. Interested in a relationship with her? Not a chance in hell.

When she's all out of options, Ella returns to her former shift at a cocktail lounge to make ends meet. Her boss is willing to give her the job back—for a price. The only thing scarier than submitting to him is being pawned off as payment to his enemies. The man who can save her is the one she should never want, but he's the only one who'd also protect her with his life.

# Chapter 1

Brent "Cobra" Rollins stalked into Anchors, fists clenched at his sides as he wove his way through the popular bar he and his Navy SEAL team frequented, not far from Naval Amphibious Base Little Creek. Low music thumped through the speakers, shot glasses slammed down on tables, and snippets of animated conversations filled the air. Howls of laughter came from a full table in the back, but Brent made a beeline for the large, sleek bar that dominated the room.

The dark polished counter seemed to stretch on for miles, with chrome and leather barstools that Brent happened to know were perfect for perching a woman on, wrapping her legs around his waist, and sinking straight into heaven.

After hours only, of course. He smirked, remembering the money he'd slipped the bartender last week. He and the pretty blonde he'd met had the place to themselves for hours. Good thing, too, because she was a screamer.

Not that he minded sending a woman straight to ecstasy. Again and again.

Specialized in it, really.

He shucked off his black leather jacket, tossing it aside as he gestured to the bartender. Row upon row of bottles lined the shelves, the mirror behind them reflecting the crowd in Anchors and making the assortment of booze seem practically infinite.

As if that would be enough liquor to get him through this fucking week.

A pretty redhead that he'd taken home a couple of weeks ago sidled up to him as he sank down onto a barstool, but he gave her a curt nod, muttering, "Not tonight, sweetheart."

A brief look of hurt flashed across her face, but she flipped her hair over her shoulders and purred, "Your loss, baby."

Brent watched her walk away, her sweet ass sashaying in those come-fuck-me heels. Hell. The woman was a tiger in bed, guaranteed to make a man beg for mercy, but he wasn't in the mood for one of his infamous one-night-stands.

Imagine that.

He ordered two shots of whiskey and downed them one right after another, the burn of the liquor chasing down his throat and searing through his veins. He ran a hand across his dark stubble and then gripped his hands together, flexing his forearms in front of him as he stretched.

Muscles rippled beneath his taut skin as some of the tension left his body from the day's brutal training, but he ignored the gawking looks of the women seated across the bar from him. At the moment he needed a stiff drink, not a quick fuck.

And since when did he turn down a willing woman?

A gorgeous babe with a spectacular rack leaned over beside him, her cloying perfume overwhelming. Her breasts practically spilled out over her low cut lacy top, and his gaze momentarily roamed there before meeting her baby blues. Hell, had he met her before? It was getting damn 'hard to keep all the women he'd taken to bed straight anymore.

"Hi Brent," she cooed in a low, sultry voice.

So that was a yes.

"Want to come back to my place tonight? I'll let you drizzle chocolate sauce all over me again."

Fuck yes. Now he remembered. Six months ago. They'd had a night for the record books—he'd licked whipped cream and chocolate from those gorgeous breasts, sucked red cherries from her wicked little mouth, and let her pleasure him with the stash of flavored condoms she had in her nightstand drawer. She was practically insatiable in the bedroom and had a spectacular body—but unfortunately her boobs were about ten times the size of her brain.

Which was why he'd left in the middle of the night without so much as a glance back. And hadn't given her a passing thought since.

"Not tonight, beautiful, I'm meeting my team in a few," he said, letting his gaze lazily roam over her.

"And I can't steal you away?"

"No can do, sweetheart."

"Are they all as tough as you?" she cooed. "Because I have a thing for big, strong military men." Her red fingernails trailed over his bicep, and Brent guffawed despite himself.

"They only wish."

"The offer is still open if you change your mind later," she said, nonchalantly palming her breasts as she stood back up.

Fucking hell. Was this chick for real?

His gaze trailed after her as his dick unwittingly rose to attention. Shit. He was here to drown his sorrows in booze and shoot the shit with his teammates, yet the whole damn female population seemed to be on the prowl tonight. Normally that was just his style, but at the moment? Not a fucking chance.

"Want a beer?" the bartender asked, raising his eyebrows as the woman sashayed away.

Brent grunted in affirmation.

He took a swig of the beer the bartender placed in front of him, his stomach churning as the date on the calendar flashed through his mind—exactly four years ago this week, his younger sister had been killed. Not in an accident, not from some debilitating illness, but from her psychopath of an ex-boyfriend.

Her ex had stalked her, unable to deal with the fact that she'd broken up with him, and then he'd followed her home late one night. Tied her up. Taken what she'd no longer freely give. Then choked the last breath from her body.

Brent had been deployed on a SEAL op with his team, halfway around the world, and his brother had been hours away working a case for the NYPD, unaware their sister was in imminent danger.

Fucking hell.

An NYPD detective and a goddamn Navy SEAL in the family, and they couldn't protect their own sister. The local police hadn't been helpful in issuing a restraining order, and he should've gone AWOL to make it home. To save her. By the time he'd requested emergency leave from his CO, it had been too late to do anything but plan a funeral.

Bile rose in his throat as he thought about her, helpless and scared, at the mercy of her murderer. The only reason the guy was still breathing was because he was rotting away in a jail cell for life. Not that that made Brent feel the slightest bit better. He was more of an "eye for an eye" kind of man. And wouldn't he goddamn love to avenge his sister. To tie that bastard up and beat the life right out of him.

No doubt his SEAL team all wondered what had crawled up his ass with the foul mood he'd been in today. They knew the story about his sister's murder but not that this week was the anniversary of her death. That the guilt fucking ate him alive most nights. He'd distract himself with an endless parade of women, burying himself night after night between a different woman's creamy thighs, but some shit just never could be reconciled.

He took another swig of his beer as the barstool beside him was suddenly jerked back.

"Yo, Cobra, what's up?" His SEAL team member Mike "Patch" Hunter sank down on the barstool next to him. "You shot out of base earlier like a bat out of hell."

Brent's gaze swept over to his teammate. "Just having a drink."

Mike meaningfully eyed the two empty shot glasses beside Brent's beer mug. "Right. And I'm a fucking girl scout."

Of course he'd noticed Brent had already started without the rest of them. All of the men were trained to be observant, but Mike seemed to have a sixth sense about things. That knowledge had proved useful on more missions than they could count. That didn't mean he wanted Mike getting on him over his shitty mood tonight though. Or guessing the reason behind it.

"Kenley's grabbing a table with the other ladies," Mike said, gesturing to the bartender for a beer.

Brent raised an eyebrow. "Ladies?"

Mike shrugged. "Everyone came here for a few drinks before we head over to the pool hall. Matthew and Evan are looking for parking spots," he said, referring to Matthew "Gator" Murphy and Evan "Flip" Jenkins, two of the other SEALs on their team.

Brent smirked. "Those are the ladies that Kenley is with?"

"Very funny, asshole. They dropped Brianna and Alison off," he said, referring to Matthew and Evan's women.

"They can't walk down the block anymore?"

"Hell, what do I know about pregnant women?"

Brent chuffed out a laugh. "You need me to teach you about the birds and the bees?"

"Fuck no. And I've got medical training for injuries in the field. I know more about limbs being blown off by IEDs than babies. Gator and Flip are probably just too overprotective for their own damn good."

"No shit," Brent agreed. "Next week they probably won't even want to hang around Anchors anymore. Too hazardous."

"Sounds about right."

Brent's gaze landed on a pretty brunette on the other side of the bar. The light pink tank top and snug-fitting jeans she had on highlighted her willowy frame, but his eyes were drawn to the perfect swell of her cleavage and gently rounded hips. Perfect for taking his mind off his troubles.

She turned away, her dark, shiny hair swishing through the air. Just the type of thing he'd love to run his fingers through. Maybe tug on a little as he tilted her head back, claiming her mouth in a kiss. Or guiding her movements as she took him into her mouth, sucking him off.

Hell.

So much for avoiding the opposite sex tonight.

His groin tightened as he watched her. Nothing like chasing after a woman who wasn't even looking his way. The other two ladies who'd approached him? Trying too damn hard. A guaranteed score. But this? She was exactly the type of challenge he needed tonight. Maybe she wasn't looking to put out, but he loved persuading many a woman to change her mind.

Mike's gaze followed his. "Thought you were going for blondes lately," he said with a chuckle.

"Since when am I particular? With a smoking body like that, she could have pink hair for all I care."

"Ain't that the goddamn truth," Matthew drawled as he grabbed the barstool on the other side of Mike. "The world keeps turning, and Brent keeps looking for an easy lay."

"She doesn't really look like your type," Mike said. "Too much clothing."

Brent chuffed out a laugh. "She's got tits and an ass. Good enough for me."

A feeling of déjà vu suddenly washed over him as he watched the brunette get change from the bartender. The glint of her gold bracelet caught his eye, and something about her seemed strikingly familiar. If she'd turn just back his way so he could get a better look at her face….

"You got a thing for Ella?" Matthew asked, eyeing the woman Brent had been watching. "Better keep your dick in your pants. Bri would kill you for sleeping with her. As a matter of fact, I would, too. Ella's way too good for your sorry ass."

Shit.

What the hell was she doing here?

"I thought she was supposed to be in college down in Florida," he said coolly.

Hell, no wonder he was fixated on her.

He'd met the gorgeous brunette weeks ago when he was down in Pensacola with his buddies but hadn't recognized her tonight from all the way across the bar. Ella had been moonlighting as a cocktail waitress as she worked her way through school. She was friends with Matthew's girl and absolutely nothing like the type of women he usually spent the night with. Nothing like the type who'd blatantly come on to him, practically begging for a night in the arms of a Navy SEAL. The kind of women he'd normally welcome into his bed.

But Ella was also the prettiest damn thing he'd ever set eyes on. Clear blue eyes, dark glossy hair, and skin that looked so soft he'd fucking love to run his hands all over it. She'd barely even glanced Brent's way that night—and that was only because he'd jumped in front of her, yelling at her asshole of a manager. The women he was used to being around would be throwing themselves at him after a move like that.

Funny thing was, he hadn't even been trying to get

her attention. His first instinct had been to shield and protect her. And possibly beat the shit out of the man who'd come charging at a defenseless woman.

"She's on spring break," Matthew said. "Came up to help Brianna get settled in."

"Is she staying with you guys?" Brent asked in disbelief.

Matthew chuffed out a laugh. "Bri just moved in with me a few days ago. No one is invited over for the next six months. At least."

Mike grinned, and the two men bumped fists.

"You two are whipped," Brent muttered.

"I'm not going to complain about waking up with a gorgeous woman in my arms every morning," Matthew said. "Hell, having Brianna in my bed is fucking spectacular."

"Best wake-up call ever," Mike agreed, waggling his eyebrows. "Although I'm usually the one waking Kenley up if you know what I mean."

Brent muttered a curse under his breath. "The whole damn bar knows what you mean."

"And to answer your question," Matthew continued, "Ella is staying with Kenley."

"At Kenley's place," Mike clarified. "Her parents still have that condo close to the beach. Kenley and I have unofficially moved in together."

"I can't keep up with this shit anymore," Brent complained. "I should go buy every last one of you a goddamn white picket fence."

"That'd look great outside our apartment door," Matthew quipped.

Brent nailed him with a glare.

It was hard to believe that one year ago every man on his SEAL team had been single. The whole team used to spend their weekends at Anchors, flirting with the pretty women and more often than not taking one home for the night. Trading stories in the locker room on Monday mornings. But the other guys had dropped like flies, each becoming involved with their current girlfriends or fiancées, until he was the last man standing. Their SEAL team leader Patrick "Ice" Foster was with Rebecca; their IT guru Christopher "Blade" Walters was engaged to Lexi; and the guys here tonight, Matthew, Mike, and Evan, also each had women of their own.

Brent wasn't into that happily-ever-after shit, but if his buddies wanted to pretend that some things lasted forever, then good luck to them.

"You guys are fucking pussy-whipped."

"We get it—the idea of you with one woman is about as likely as hell freezing over," Matthew said.

"I'm not about to let a woman lead me around, dick in my hand."

The men on their team were protective and possessive as hell. Dedicated to their country and their careers. Apparently that trait carried over into their relationships as well. Once they found their woman, that was it. Not that he planned to ever test those waters himself.

His alcoholic father had left when he was a kid. His single mother raised him and his siblings the best that she could. But when his sister was murdered by her ex-boyfriend, when Brent had received her frantic calls and messages the week before and hadn't been able to get home to her in time, it had almost destroyed him.

Even today the guilt practically ate him alive.

The idea of not being able to protect those that he

loved burned through him. Rage clawed at his chest. Pushing himself harder and harder in training and losing himself in a woman night after night were about the only ways he could deal with the reality. He just couldn't handle losing someone like that again. Ever. If he didn't get close to anyone, he couldn't get burned.

No fault in that logic.

"You can't keep up with us?" Mike laughed, drawing Brent's gaze back toward him. "At least we're with the same woman every night. There's gotta be like ten women you've slept with here in Anchors tonight."

"Don't remind me," Brent muttered. Normally he'd be the first to brag about the women he'd been with, offering up all the sordid details to his buddies. The amount of pussy he'd scored. At the moment, however, it was just a grim reminder of the fact that he couldn't fucking live with the guilt without distracting himself with a woman. Or twenty.

Mike raised his eyebrows. "What bit you in the ass?"

"Just having an off night."

"You're losing your touch, Cobra," Matthew said, calling him by his nickname. "Three drinks in, and there's still not a woman at your side being seduced by your charm?"

"A woman?" Mike laughed. "Usually he's got an entire posse of them."

"Just needed to clear my head," Brent muttered.

Matthew raised his eyebrows, and Brent drained the last of his beer, catching a reflection of the women in the mirror that stretched across the back of the bar.

Matthew's fiancée Brianna was laughing, her blonde hair shimmering under the lights. Evan was animatedly telling a story, his strawberry-blonde girlfriend Alison smiling beside him. They all laughed again, and Brent's eyes roved over the group. Why they'd all come here before heading off to the pool hall was beyond him.

But that wasn't what had him clenching his fists in frustration.

Ella.

She stood up, her glossy, dark hair swinging through the air. Bright blue eyes lit up as she smiled at the others, her face slightly flushed. The tank top she had on highlighted her small but supple breasts, and her jeans clung to hips a man would love to wrap his hands around as he tugged her closer. Palmed her ass. And buried himself deep within her tight heat.

Hell.

She was wearing more clothing than half of the women here, but the curve-hugging jeans and form-fitting top she had on were sexy-as-fuck.

And making him harder than steel.

A couple of dudes at the table next to them all looked her way, and Brent ground his teeth together. One of the men walked over, apparently interested in her, and she shook her head 'no.'

Well thank fuck for that.

He didn't want to have to bust some frat boy's balls for touching Ella.

She shouldn't even be here since she lived down in Florida. Their paths never even should've crossed. But the gorgeous brunette fascinated him. Aroused him. Made him want to beat to a pulp any man that came near her. Especially that shitty manager of hers.

Her face had been etched in his brain ever since the night they first met. Which was kind of crazy considering he'd been with countless other women. He could barely keep their faces straight despite knowing their bodies intimately, and he hadn't so much as touched Ella.

But her long, dark hair, those big blue eyes, and that lithe little body with curves in just the right places had made his pulse pound. Not to mention that just the sight of her had sent his protective, possessive instincts surging to the surface. He'd stood up to her asshole manager down in Florida the first time they'd met.

And seeing her again tonight?

He had all sorts of images running through his head of kissing her pink lips, moving his mouth down the slender column of her neck. Maybe bending her over a table, taking her from behind while he cupped her small breasts. Showing her just how crazy she made him. Making her moan his name.

God.

What would it be like to thrust into her pussy while he massaged her breasts and sank his teeth into the tender flesh where her neck and shoulder joined? She was so goddamn young. Unaffected by him. Still in college while he was thirty-two. And he had no doubt that he could pleasure her beyond her wildest imagination.

"Shall we go join the ladies?" Mike asked, jarring him out of his thoughts.

Brent glanced over to see his buddy draining the last of his beer.

"Hell yeah. They're much better company than this sorry ass," Matthew joked, punching Brent in the shoulder as he stood up. "Better looking, too."

Fucking idiot. The most Matthew had to worry about was moving his gorgeous fiancée in with him and picking out new bedding and shit. Buying a few baby clothes for the kid they had on the way. He hadn't lost someone in his own family. Failed to protect his own sister.

"I'll meet you guys there," Brent muttered.

Maybe a ride on his Harley down to the pool hall would clear his head.

Watching his friends play happily-ever-after sure wasn't going to erase the nightmares in his head. Maybe he should've left earlier with one of those women. The redhead, the other one—what the hell did it matter? It figured that the one woman who'd piqued his interest tonight was the one he shouldn't fucking touch.

He'd lost track of his conquests over the years, and the number was almost something to be ashamed of. Almost. Because he didn't answer to anyone but himself. And there was something exhilarating about pleasuring a woman—discovering her body, learning her secrets, making her whimper and beg and cry out his name. He was a goddamn master at sending a woman straight to ecstasy. And if a woman beneath him made him forget for a couple of hours about all of his failures and gave him sweet release as well, then that was just the cherry on top.

So why the hell was he still sitting here at Anchors with his buddies and not rolling around in the sheets?

His fists clenched as Ella's face once again flashed through his mind.

Damn it to hell.

<u>Now Available in Paperback!</u>